THE INFIRM

for Lucy

THE INFIRM

Russell Helms

A standard-issue backpack held the necessary supplies for Lura's round of home visits—clippers, an
emery board, hydrogen peroxide, and small bandag-
es, should she draw blood.

Lura's oval face broke into a bright smile when
needed, but mostly she held it in neutral, neither
showing nor hiding her very straight teeth. Her
short hair, the color of dust and parted in the middle, bounced as she walked. She wore a light blue
outfit, loose and suited to the climate-controlled en-
vironment, kept at a moderate 72 degrees. Through
the dome, a cold winter sun sent its rays in, soaking
the stacked concrete homes and steel buildings.
The lane empty and quiet, she came to building
8487 and entered through a low arch to the elevator.
There were twenty-one units on three levels, and
she would visit them all. She passed the elevator
and entered a hall paved with artificial marble,
skeins of fake color shot throughout. At the first
door, she paused, listened, and held her badge to a
scanner there. The door clicked and hummed open.
Lura stepped inside, smelling shit, and felt her day
getting longer.

"Lord, get in here, girl," said Mrs. Tubman, using her artificial voice.

Lura kept a straight face and gazed at Dottie
Tubman in her electric wheelchair. She was canted
back, looking at the white ceiling. Dottie weighed
exactly 342 pounds, 11 ounces. Her face was sallow
and deathly white, as white as milk. A roll of fat
squeezed her eyes into little prunes, and she darted
them this way and that. She wore a skin suit, laven-

der, with her fat feet shoved into fuzzy blue slippers. She still had her arms and legs, but was otherwise hopeful.

"Hey there, baby," said Lura. She was slight, an even 120 pounds, and as unblemished by disease and distress as they come.

Dottie's chair twirled in the open room as she eased it in front of a low stool where Lura would sit.

"What's cooking?"

Lura laughed. She had to get her pleasures from the small things. "You had your Scrumptious today?" She checked the Scrumptious bin, and it was empty.

"Yes, honey. I done ate, girl. But I sure am hungry. Can you punch me down another brick?"

Lura hit the red button. Within seconds, a whoosh, and there it was. Dottie could still chew, which was a source of shame, but she just couldn't get up the nerve to get the permanent feeding tube or have her teeth pulled. What if something went wacko? There were stories.

Lura retrieved the salmon-colored brick that was stamped into break-apart cubes. "Yum, yum, and more yum," said Lura. She hated the Scrumptious and saved all of her spare earnings, meager as they were, to buy little treats, specially flavored Scrumptious with different textures. "Here comes the airplane!" She zoomed a cube into Dottie's mouth.

Dottie frowned at that but had to chew versus complain. She wasn't a child after all. "For Pete's sake. Get me some water, bitch." She laughed that laugh that said, "I'm just poking fun."

Lura put her hands on her hips. "With a tube, I could just push the water in, no swallowing. You ever thought of that?"

"I don't think they pay you to think, little girl," said Dottie. To her, everybody was little girl or little boy, especially the walkers, the Uprights, the fucking mobile, the perambulators, damn them to hell.

"Shut your face and chew," said Lura. She poked another cube into Dottie's gaping mouth. She drew down a tumbler of warm water from the wall tap and held it to Dottie's prim mouth, two thin lines embedded in fleshy jelly.

Dottie swallowed her Scrumptious, sucked her teeth, and slurped some water. "Dammit, I can hold the damn cup. Give it to me."

"Oh, what you can and what you can't do," said Lura. She gazed around the single room, the toilet and vacuum tube in the corner. On the wall was a twenty-by-twenty photo of the Great One, eyes crossed, lips wet, his watermelon head easing out of the frame. The Chatty was off, the little red light glowing in and out, and resting.

Lura inserted the fourth and final cube into Dottie's pouty mouth, let her chew, and then proffered the water once more. Done, and Dottie belched a good one.

"Onward, bitch!" said Dottie. "It's been a long seven days. I been counting 'em down. I can feel 'em growing. Oh, dear Lord, will you rub 'em first?"

"All in good time," said Lura, "but I smell shit. Got to empty that bag, dear sweet precious baby."

She ran the suction tube to the chair. She pulled up Dottie's silvery top and eyeballed the full bag of liquid stool and urine. "Just about to rupture." She inserted the tube and hit go, sucking the bag clean without losing a single drop. "Flat as a flitter!" She hit an overhead spray button and freshened the room, kind of like oatmeal with butter and brown sugar, whatever that was.

Next, Lura sat on the acrylic stool and pulled the chair a bit closer. "Let's see what we got, big mama." She pulled off the houseshoes that fit like gloves. "Ho! Yellow and crunchy, no doubt. You ready, big mama?"

Dottie made a clucking noise and wiggled her nine toes, one lost to diabetes. Getting the go-ahead for insulin was one of her proudest memories.

Lura took her toenail shears and went from smallest to biggest, little puffs of dead powder popping with each clip. She had a mask, but it made her feel lightheaded. The index toe was ingrown, and she used the clippers to lift the nail's tip. It cracked and puffed. With her fingers, Lura peeled the jagged nail sideways, tearing it down to the quick. A dot of blood peeped out. Lura imagined that it made a little squeal, happy to be apart from its host.

The big toe was next, the nail thick and extending a good half inch. Lura reached into her bag and pulled out the wire cutters. She snipped and cracked, little bits flying. "Just like a damn piece of glass," said Lura. She laughed.

The Chatty blooped on, the button on the back of Dottie's eyetooth having been pushed with her tongue. She longed for the day when all things possible would rest within her mouth.

Lura moved on to foot two, four toes, and made quick business of it. "There, you old so and so. Let me see them claws." She took Dottie's hand and started over. It took a few minutes, her attention wandering to the Chatty, a cute ditty being sung by a little girl who was holding her spine in a sack in her lap. "That's all, folks!" and the screen switched to the Great One, drooling onto a satin cloth emblazoned with the single yellow star. Lura stood and saluted, her face in a smirk.

"Okay, Dottie, girl, you been good today. What else can I do you for?" Lura shifted onto one leg, her hand like a tea spout.

Dottie lifted her arm, as if defeated, and waved her off. Her voice box ground. "Enough with you, baby. Be on your way." She had ideas to keep her isolation number high, her score competing with the others of 8487. She'd learn them a trick or two.

Lura gathered her tools, rinsed them in the tiny sink with peroxide, and then washed her hands. *Forward!*

Three hours later, Lura emerged from 8487, her back aching, her hands chapped from the washing. She couldn't afford to have an infection on her record, too costly. The sun was overhead, bleeding through the milky-white dome, and she made her way to the showers, wondering if he would be there.

~

The showers were only two blocks from Lura's flat at 6800. Her place was just a single room, eighty square feet, with a slim bed, a sink, a Scrumptious bin, and a toilet against the wall. A tight carpet of brown and half of a wall devoted to the Chatty, which ran continuously on a single channel for the Uprights, live coverage of the Great One in his reclining wheelchair, or on a fuzzy blanket, his mouth wet, his eyes blank stares. He was the Great One due to his curious combination of cerebral palsy, hydrocephaly, diabetes, Tay-Sachs, four-limb amputation (his parents were rich), and torticollis, which wrenched his massive head to the left. A fine down of red hair covered the top of his gelatinous head like peach fuzz. He breathed on his own, ster-torously, but all faithful were looking for artificial life support as his next step up the rung of infamy, that and autism. Dialysis to boot.

This particular shower, a gray building with a flashing S, occupied half a city block. As Lura drew closer, other Uprights appeared, passing through the revolving gate. Without so much as a peep, the line moved forward. Lura kept a distance of two feet between herself and the Upright before her. She recognized him, suspected he worked in the 8300s. His broad shoulders blocked her view, but what was there to see except a staircase heading down, the ground level holding a variety of pets and pooches that made visits to the almighty Infirm. That would be on Friday.

Lura passed through the scanner and clucked her tongue with lips closed. No speaking allowed. The showers were oddly soothing, although sterile and tepid. In the hallway were screens of the Great

One. Lura gazed at his sad face, his lolling eyes, his angry shoulder and hip stumps doused in baby powder. At midnight, live video of Uprights licking his privates, their ecstatic looks of joy, his member tiny and shriveled like a frog.

Lura passed through the revolving gate and glanced at the number there, 72. She entered the antechamber and stepped out of her blue uniform, pulled down her underwear, the pad there in her panties, which she peeled and dropped into a basket. In front of her, a naked man, his mark on his back between his shoulder blades. He stepped into the carousel, and she followed, leaning back into the cold rubberized steel.

The carousel clanked, gathering forty-eight Uprights in a circle, and the wash began, a rinse of warm water followed by streaming globs of sudsy soap. Lura lathered her body, her face, her hair, her sex parts, and the carousel jerked, sending the cadre into a slow spin of still more water. She took care to keep her legs spread, to get a good rinse, and that was that, the carousel unwinding into a straight line, a draft sending chills across her chest, her nipples erect. She stepped out, as did the others, and walked forward through the drying tunnel, wiping water from her eyes. The drying passage doubled back, then went up again. The line re-formed, and she entered the dressing room, where she took clean panties, a new pad, and a top and bottom. The camera's eye, and the Infirm all around the sequestered city watched with impatience on channel three, waiting for something, perhaps a fight, perhaps a rape, anything to dull the passing hours.

Just the sound of feet in flimsy slippers scuffing the smooth cement, the Uprights ascending the stairs, the plaintive echoes, headed to their flats.

Lura emerged from the shower facility onto the somewhat sunshiny street. She could find her flat with eyes closed, and she walked, the crowd thinning, the smell of lemon soap dissipating from her brethren. He hadn't been there, and she wondered as she walked, eager for home and the surprise in her Scrumptious bin. She passed rows of Upright tenements, a mimosa tree growing in a huge pot, and crossed the lane. Two others were entering her building, and she gave them space, slowing so that her walk up the stairs would continue in solitary silence. The surprise, she longed for, and she scanned herself into her tiny flat. The Chatty brightly lighting the space, the Great One drooling on a pillow, a soft voice narrating the scene, mostly non-sequiturs, puns: *Bite the cigar. Really clamp down on that motherfucker!*

Rather than check the bin and be disappointed, she sat, gathering her nerve. The night would be so long otherwise, and now a new beanie was being placed on the Great One's giant head, hand-knit from a viewer in Tacoma, Washington: *Descartes was a philosopher. Draycart was a wagon.* A close-up of the alabaster skin, the blue veins, the poof of red hair. His neck was drawn, the cords there tight as piano wires. The camera panned to his genitals, a little flabby knob, the testicles undescended.

Thirsty, Lura went to the sink and drank two

glasses. She couldn't help herself and glanced into the Scrumptious bin. Would there be Champy? The little brick of cubes was there, the Scrumptious, her dinner, and the flap to the tube was just ajar. Perhaps there was something behind it? Lura lifted the flap of thin metal, and there it was, a small package wrapped in white paper. Would she be up all night hallucinating, or would she fall into a stupor and sleep like the dead? One never knew, but came to rely on the mini-vacations provided by Champy, fizzy and lemon-flavored. Just holding the package gave her a little thrill. It was only after two, and she made herself wait. What to do? She'd already scanned in and couldn't leave until seven the next morning, bath and lunch day. Again, she thought of him, imagined him, tall, lanky, his neck thin and smooth, deep brown hair. Were his eyes green? She couldn't remember. There was a bit of stoop to his gait, but he came across as healthy and strong. His face, most of all, registered a wan kindness, as if he was burdened for humankind but settled on some temporary solution.

The hands on the screen were pulling aside the Great One's butt cheeks, and the camera sank into the scene, an everted anus, angry and red. *Oh, praise the Great One! The alphabet sought counseling. White butterflies skim the lawn!* Lura imagined shoving a stick of dynamite in there. She'd read about dynamite on library day, which was Friday. Knowledge kept her further from Infirm status, and the Infirm really did need her, really did need to keep her healthy despite the grossness of it all. *Poor pitiful*

Uprights! That's where she'd met him, at the library, and she wondered what his favorite books were.

Lura gazed at the blank tan wall around the Chatty. The glow of light from the ceiling. On the other side of the wall was Merriman, a strapping man of fifty with a bit of a belly. She wondered if he'd received the Champy, wondered if he'd been as lucky. She turned her chair with her foot and faced the opposite wall, the sink and toilet there. On the other side was a big-boned woman, Wanda, who had a ready smile, but with wrinkled, worried eyes. Lura raised her feet, and the chair revolved on its own, bringing her back to the screen.

The Great One's leg nubs, amputated nearly to the hips, the scars barely visible, the skin red and irritated. *Oh Glorious! The wolf licked its cold sore. A farmer who heats his house (beats his horse).*

Lura glanced at her closed door. No one ever knocked there, and she often daydreamed about receiving a visitor, perhaps even an Infirm. She calculated that she'd formed at least ten thousand words in her head that day, and no one to gift them to, other than the rigmarole of work chatter. Some could talk, but the lucky ones had severed vocal cords.

Lura jumped. The screen had blacked out, and then it was a News Flash! She gripped her thighs and listened. It was him, the guy from the library, his mug shot, left, right, and front. A soothing voice announced that he had violated an Infirm, that he was missing, and that he was Jack. A tiny thrill turned to a spasm and caught her breath. The penalty would be death no less, she knew. There were no further details, just the repeating views of his face, his calm and kind face. The voice issued a calm warning, offering a week's Champy to anyone with information. Lura stood. God, where could he be? It was nearly impossible to hide, scanners and hover-heads following the progress of the Upright throughout the day, keeping meticulous records. Lura put her head into her hands and noticed the wetness there. The Great One reappeared. *Translators sharing cigarettes. The fluff of egg.*

After pacing for a full ten minutes, Lura couldn't take it anymore and retrieved her Champy. She dropped the lozenge into a glass of water and watched the fizz, inhaling the lemony vapor. She sat on her bed and drank deeply.

~

Earlier that day, Jack had entered 9323 and begun his rounds of foot care, his mind dim with the lack of possibilities. His third Infirm of the day, a character by the name of Chet Spurlock, a judge, proved challenging as usual. Dialysis had not gone well, and he was grumpy. The brain tumor was developing as planned, but gave him tremendous headaches. Chet had a habit of snapping his fingers, and that's what got Jack the most.

"I said lick my balls." Chet's lazy eye rolled from wall to wall.

Jack focused on clipping the littlest toenail, his blood rising. Sex day was Sunday. This was Monday, foot-care day. He'd licked the judge's balls the day before and still had the sour taste in his mouth.

"You deaf, boy!" The Chatty played an ad for Scrumptious.

"Yessir, I've gone deaf," said Jack. He imagined the wire cutters in his backpack.

"Well, you can wish all you want, boy. You're just an Upright, so don't get sassy with me." Chet wore a thin green gown, and the AC clicked on with a gentle hum.

Jack massaged the judge's big toe, his face red. He surveyed the judge's flaccid thighs. "Okay, sir, you want me to lick your balls, sir? Your wish is my command." He retrieved the wire cutters and laid them on the footstool. "Gotta get that ingrown nail first. But, here, let me get you ready." He lifted Chet's gown, reached in between the squeezed thighs, and scooped out his dick and balls. "There we go."

"Now we're talking. Big money!" said the judge. He leaned back in his reclining chair, gripping the rails with his lobster-claw hands, just a big thumb and a single finger, and closed his eyes.

"Yessir," said Jack. On his knees, he was four feet tall. "Well, let's get to it." He picked up the wire cutters. He went and kissed the judge's balls, almost spat, and then grabbed the whole package and choked it. In went the wire snips, and the judge howled, coming straight up, his eyes on fire. Jack held on tight and attacked the rising flesh, ripping through it, not feeling the lobster claws beat his head. The judge screamed bloody murder, but Jack was of one mind and stabbed and tore until a bloody mess of flesh was in his hands.

Before he passed out, the judge had lifted and

careened onto the thinly carpeted floor, blood gushing from his stump. Jack took the bloody mess and forced it into the judge's mouth, grimacing at the bloody horror of it all. A sense of peace came over him, and then he knew that he had to run. Behind him, the Chatty played porn from the day before, a handjob.

Jack hurried to the sink, the judge screaming on the floor. He washed his hands and paused at the blood beneath his nails. There was nothing in the backpack that would help, and he left it there, scanning his card to exit and entering the long hallway. On the walls was art, a pencil sketch of a colostomy. He walked to the stairs and scanned to exit the building. He was to scan at every corner, but dropped his card. He would be a wanted man as soon as he missed the first scan. He ran with a plan in mind, but slowed when he encountered a group of Infirm in wheelchairs. He doffed an imaginary hat and headed to the first Upright housing block in his path, 6800. He waited at the front door. Soon, a middle-aged woman walked up, her eyes wide. He stepped aside, and she scanned and entered with Jack on her heels.

"Don't worry. I have clearance," said Jack. "I need…"

The woman trotted away, looking over her shoulder.

Jack watched her disappear into a room and knew that he'd lost his chance. "Fuck." He took the stairs to the third floor and began knocking on doors.

A door opened just a crack and then shut. He moved to the next with the same result. At the next door, he knocked in a slow, calm manner, put a smile on his face, and said a practice hello, his heart beating wildly.

Lura was hallucinating on her bed, a jungle of vines twisted around dead chickens. She sat up and imagined a door in the dense vegetation. Someone was knocking. Suddenly, there were many doors, too many to count, and she opened them one at a time.

Jack waited, ready to head to the next door, and the door opened. He jammed his foot in the space, but the door flew open and hit a woman, sending her to the floor. "Oh, my god, I'm sorry." He closed the door and knelt beside her. She was squirming and mouthing, and he recognized the effects of Champy. And it was her.

Lura rolled onto her stomach and crawled toward the bed, pulling herself up with vines. Weird bugs with soft, flappy wings flopped, and she shooed them away.

Jack watched her collapse onto her stomach. He pulled down the collar of her shirt and saw the mark there. Her name was Lura. He took her limp body and turned it over, recognizing her from the library and the shower. He put the pillow beneath her head, waiting for her to scream, but she was silent, breathing deeply with a queer look on her face. He glanced at the Chatty and smirked. A close-up of the Great One's red and watery left eye. *She lost thirty pounds on a diet of tendons and ligaments. Goddamn you is not a suggestion!*

Shaking now, Jack surveyed the small room and spied the Scrumptious in the tray. He took half and wolfed it down, followed by a glass of water. What next? He sat in the chair, turned toward the bed, and watched Lura as she seethed spit between her teeth, and her hands trembled.

~

Waking with his parts in his mouth, the judge gagged. He hit the panic button on his tooth with his tongue, and his Chatty became a two-way monitor. The face of a bored cleric appeared, but boredom gave way to alarm.

"I've been...mauled! The bloody motherfucker! Help me! God dammit, help me!"

The armless cleric had hit record with her head wand and surveyed the judge's bloody mouth. "Help is on the way, sir!" The cleric checked the judge's coordinates and dispatched emergency. "Hold on, sir! Help is on the way, sir!"

"Oh, I'm ruined!" said the judge. "Hurry, please hurry." He dared not look at his crotch, but pressed his fist there, feeling the wetness. His vision blared, and he passed out once again.

The cleric kept the live video open, watching, waiting. Within five minutes, a team of three Uprights from the hospital screeched to a halt in front of the building in a golf cart ambulance. The report was of a stabbing, unheard of among the Infirm.

The three bounded up the stairs and cracked the door with an emergency pass. The judge lolled on the floor, turning side to side, his eyes rolled back, muttering.

"Holy freak show," said the lead medic. The other two rushed to the judge's side, his gown around his waist, the bloody mess of his privates showing. His rank would most definitely rise, but pissing would be a problem.

~

Jack stared at Lura. He knew that the Champy would keep her high through the night, as she traveled from dream to dream. Occasionally, she moaned, her fingers flexing, her feet twitching. He checked the Scrumptious bin to make sure there wasn't more Champy, but it was empty. He lifted the flap and felt with his fingers. Nothing. The Infirm could summon Scrumptious and Champy at will. He cursed the day he was born normal. He'd always known he would wind up hurting someone, and had worked out a vague plan to escape outside the dome. Only a third of the city had been domed for a few hundred years. Outside, there was an extensive network of roads, tunnels, and sewers. He would have to find his way to the edge and, with any luck, a sewer opening.

He kept his face turned from the Chatty, wondering how this Lura could possibly help him. She would no doubt be held complicit and executed, slowly dissected on live-feed video, channel 12. He owed this woman something, plus she was attractive, reminding him of his lonely life. Perhaps it was just best to be caught and killed, but now he had this other life on his hands. "Come on, Jack, think, think." He pulled at his brown hair in frustration. It would be dark soon. Better to escape in the dark.

There would be room-to-room searches, no doubt, and prior to that, video looks through the Chatty. If he pressed himself to the wall beside the screen, he could just fit, perhaps remain undetected. "Think!" He went there and drew in his shoulders, but couldn't stay still. *Hell, just let them catch me.* They would send Uprights, Squad, loyal to the cause, eager to please.

Lura sat up in bed, swaying from side to side. In her visions, she'd seen the guy from the library. He was behind a thick wooden door covered in lichen, and she had opened it. She stared, and he was there, sitting in her chair. She blinked and propped herself, wishing away the visions for something real. She spoke.

"You're here. You've come. But why?" Behind him, she watched a rainbow swallow itself color by color.

"Holy cow," said Jack. "You're talking. We've met at the library, in the shower. Can you hear me?" He leaned forward in the chair.

Lura strained to focus, not wanting to lose her buzz, afraid that the apparition would disappear. But what if it was real? She'd never hallucinated an Upright before.

"Who...are you? How did you get here?" said Lura, slurring her words.

"You opened the door. I'm Jack. I'm real. The Champy is working on you, but you've broken through."

"But...why?" She fell back to one elbow.

"They're looking for me, Central that is. I hurt

an Infirm, but for good reason. He had it coming, and now I need to escape to the outside."

"Oh, that's fucked up. They'll catch you. Burn you alive. Put it on the Chatty." She wavered, her head as if on a ball joint. "You can't stay here..." There was a lion making love to a puma, and Komodo dragons eating eggs containing human embryos.

"Lura, your name is Lura. Do you have any passes I could use? Maybe a vacation pass?"

"Oh, God, I can't think." The human embryos bursting from the guts of the Komodo dragons, making love to the lions. "But then they'll think it's me. They'll kill me. Oh, God, what have you done?" She fell to her back, groaning.

"Look, you want out of here as much as I do. We've met, and that can't be undone. We can escape together. Can you walk?"

"No."

"Then I can carry you. I'll carry you, run with you, saying that I'm taking you to the hospital. Maybe that's the break we'll need."

Human embryos in a giant skillet, the whites cooking. "Oh, God. Just go. I can't..."

"We have to try. Do you like living here? Here, try to stand. I'll pick you up and carry you over my shoulder." He took her limp hand, pulled her upright. "You read adventure, right?"

"Oh, God." Lura felt herself standing and then flopped like a wet rag across his broad shoulder.

Jack wobbled to the door and opened it without scanning an ID. He would have to hurry and stumbled into the empty hall. He struggled with her down the stairs, passing an older gentleman, his jaw agape.

"She's hurt. Going to the hospital!" He pushed through the glass door and into the street, headed for the park six blocks away. To everyone he met, it was the same. "She's hurt, going to the hospital!"

He passed building after building, and a clamor reached him. Ahead, a dozen Infirm in wheelchairs coming down the street. Jack slowed and avoided eye contact, turning at the first intersection. It wouldn't be an Infirm who caught him but one of their goddamn Upright flunkies. Squad.

"Whuh, whuh...can't breathe," said Lura.

"Shit. I'm sorry." Jack shifted her into a fireman's carry, feeling her warm body pressing into his. "Just stay with me. So far so good."

~

Central was hopping. This was the first castration they'd had in over a decade. Colonel Faccia looked at the data: the names of the Upright not in their flats or properly scanned on the streets, the Uprights checked into the homes of the Infirm. There were two unaccounted for, and one was Jack. He'd been assigned to the building where Chet Spurlock lived. But then there was one other. Lura. But what was the connection with Lura?

Squad descended on the city, looking for the tall and lanky Jack. On electric mopeds, a team of thirty hummed the streets, little blue lights baubling on the handlebars. On the Chatty, photos of the two popped up all around the city. Within minutes, everyone knew, the Uprights cheering on the unlikely heroes.

~

Sweating and huffing, Jack made it to the park and its narrow flat lanes, wide enough for a wheelchair. Not many were about, and Jack trotted, Lura bouncing on his shoulders. Throngs of gecko trees, and he left the path, soon invisible. Exhausted, he stopped and slid Lura to the ground.

"Whuh?" said Lura. She looked up through the canopy of limbs and leaves. Each was dotted with a giant red ant, shooting fire.

"We're okay," said Jack. "Just have to rest. There's a road. I've been there plenty of times."

Leaning against a tree, Lura weaved in and out of consciousness. Green gorillas, roses made of cement. She just wanted to close her eyes and be taken away by the visions. She listened to Jack's fast, deep breaths. She couldn't remember how they'd met. Why were they in the park? Did she know him? Hadn't she recognized him from the library?

Jack glanced at his watch. Seven minutes had passed. "We have to go. Can you walk now?"

Lura's eyes were closed. Velvet baby blankets covered her body, so warm and soft. Without waiting for a reply, Jack kneeled and hoisted her again to his shoulders, walking toward the edge, the perimeter of thirty feet near the end of the dome's base. He looked up and could see the slope of the dome growing closer to the ground, a dull blue sky. The fence would be up ahead, and he bore right to intersect a road.

Sweating and straining with Lura, he soon came

to foundations of old buildings torn down hundreds of years ago. There would be a road, and he found it, a two-lane, crumbling asphalt covered with leaves and debris, with curbs of cement. He looked for manhole covers or drains into the sewers below. Lura's weight seemed ready to crush him, and he lowered her to the littered street.

"Whuh?" said Lura. She focused on the pair of legs in front of her and looked up. The hallucinations were fading, "You. Jack? You hurt somebody."

"Come on, get up. Have to find an opening to the sewer. For now, we're in this together...I apologize for dragging you into this." He pulled her up by her hands. He steadied her. "Okay, let's walk, sister."

Lura realized that her life had changed forever, but it might as well be with this Jack. What else did she have except the damned Infirm? She gazed at his short brown hair, his smooth, thin neck. She walked, supported by his arm. He scuffed the layers of dirt and leaves from the road, looking for the manhole cover. Junk trees grew inside the foundations of old buildings and to the edge of the road. A moldy smell.

For ten minutes, they walked, Jack kicking through the layered detritus. His toe caught the edge of something. "Here!" He sat Lura on the low curb, and she wobbled there. He dug with his feet, revealing the round metal cover. *Made in USA* stamped into a grid pattern. There were slots to insert a pry bar. He dug in his fingers, but it wouldn't budge. He wiped the sweat from his eyes, looking, listening.

~

Squad, dressed in gray jumpsuits with black stripes down the side, descended first on Jack's flat and then Lura's. The video from Lura's place showed Jack entering, then carrying her out. He would be easy to catch, and half of Squad searched the city while the other half made for the outskirts. A team of three headed to the city park, first checking the lanes and wheelchair trails. They fanned out toward the dome's perimeter.

Jack removed a piece of steel rebar from an old parking barrier. Prying the edge of the manhole cover open, he slid the bar in. Using his fingers, he hefted the heavy round of metal and let it fall, wincing at the sound. His back ached. His head pounded. He lay on his stomach, looking into the hole. There was an old steel ladder leading down. A dank smell of rotting leather. He said his name, listening to the echo. He glanced at Lura sitting on the curb and was overcome by how attractive Lura was. Her skin perfect, her face smooth and oval. He imagined running with her to the ends of the earth.

Twenty feet apart and pressing forward, three Squad stumbled onto the old foundations. Using his radio, Chuck called for his comrades to join him on the road. There were scuff marks and what looked like footprints in the thick layers of leaves and dirt. Armed with stun guns, the three marched, scrub growing in the middle of the road.

Jack could feel his pursuers and imagined he would be discovered at any moment. A chill washed his body. He helped Lura to the hole. "You have to climb down. Okay?"

Lura looked down at her feet and was overcome with dizziness, and sank to her knees. "I can't."

"Yes, you can. You have to. You'll be executed otherwise." And then, in the distance, he saw them, heads and torsos. "Shit!" He scrambled into the hole, holding on with one hand. With the other, he guided Lura's legs. "In, get in!"

"Hey!" yelled Chuck, and the pursuers broke into a run.

Jack watched Squad, bounding toward them. There was only one thing to do. He had no other choice. "Hey, I'm going down. Follow if you can." Down in the hole, he looked up at her face peering down at him. She spoke, and he wondered if what he heard was true. Without looking again, he descended the ladder into the darkness, a square shaft about ten feet wide. It was dry, and he ran as fast as he could, his hand trailing the wall beside him, a feeling of disgust and longing filling his gut.

~

At the jail, Chuck personally handed over his prize, Lura. It was 4 p.m.

"Well, well," said the head jailer, Marty. He looked like a balloon with legs, somewhat halfway between Infirm and Upright. "What do you have to say for yourself, you piece of trash."

Lura's head spun. Brief flashes. A giant birthday cake. Cannibals eating breakfast. "He kidnapped me, that's all. I need to sit down."

"Sit her down, maybe she'll talk," said Marty. His voice was high and whiny. "So why would he kidnap you? You were in on this all along, right?"

Her guards sat her on a bench against the smooth gray wall. The room was small with just a desk. A steel door with a tiny window.

"The Champy. I had no idea what was happening. He just took me."

"And that's no excuse. Why would he just randomly select you to be his accomplice? There has to be something more, and we'll find that out in due time, missy. The dome is highly displeased. The Great One will be unhappy when he hears of this and will want justice, no doubt." Marty cackled.

"I need to sleep. The Champy," said Lura.

"Always the Champy, isn't it? I don't know why we pleasure you fools with that garbage."

"It's all we have," said Lura.

"We give you a nice room with a view of the Great One. We feed you twice a day. What more could you want?"

Lura's chin was touching her chest. She shook her head.

"Okay, lock her up, boys," said Marty. "If she's out for mercy, she's highly mistaken."

"Stand, prisoner," said Chuck. He and another guard pulled her up. Another opened the door, and soon Lura was in a tiny cell with a narrow bed, a toilet, and large Chatties in the hall.

Lura fell back on the bunk, her head on the thin pillow. She closed her eyes to sleep and fell into a long dream, dreaming of Jack and the hole in the road.

~

One Squad had entered the sewer, spooked, but could not see and withdrew. Every few hundred feet, Jack stopped to listen. His watch glowed in the dark, and after two hours of walking in blindness, he stopped and slid down against the wall. Something brushed his neck, and he swiped at it. Rumor was that giant spiders lived in the sewers, that and bloodthirsty rats. He had no idea what a rat might look like, but he imagined all head and teeth. He felt something on his leg and jumped up, hitting himself there. He wanted to scream. Instead, he thought about the judge, Chet Spurlock, how he had snipped his parts off and shoved them into his mouth. If he were caught, might he not end up in front of the same?

He broke into a jog, feeling that he would smash his head against an overhang. For nearly half an hour, he plunged through the darkness, then, up ahead, saw a very faint beam of light that grew brighter and brighter. He slowed to a walk and soon came to the source. There was a ladder and above it a manhole cover slightly ajar. He took a deep breath, climbed the ladder, and pressed with one hand. The heavy steel plate barely moved. Feeling that his life depended on escaping the endless sewer, he pushed again. For twenty minutes, he pushed and finagled the cover until it was halfway clear. Bending his head down, he took a step up and pressed with the back of his neck and shoulders. The lid lifted and clapped back down, showering him with black dirt.

"Fuck."

Again, he pushed and forced himself up with his legs, the cover rising and then collapsing onto its side with a thud. The light blinded him, and he crawled out dazed. Here, there were no gingko trees, but tall pines. A thick mat of pine straw covered the ground, peppered with cones. He stood and looked around. No buildings. No foundations. Just the pines and a few holly bushes with pointy leaves. He looked down at his pants leg, a black spider there as big as his hand, and he leaped and swung his leg against a tree. He yelled, feeling that he'd broken his shin and hopped backward, tripping over a stump, watching the crippled spider scurry away.

"Fuck!" He imagined his small, cozy room and wished he were there. He had no food or water and felt weak. "Well, what's next?" The air was cold, the sunlight beginning to wane. He shivered and limped along what he thought of as a road that followed the sewer beneath him. He had no idea what to expect, except that another dome was nearby, the dimly known Laramore.

After an hour of walking, he came to a small creek and was amazed. He had heard of water running like this and had imagined it would be filthy and filled with mud, but this was clear water running over smooth stones. He kneeled beside the creek, soaking his pants, and put his lips to it, tasting and then slurping and slurping until he felt his stomach would burst. Thoroughly chilled, his shivering soon turned to shaking. The only thing he could do was keep moving.

~

Tuesday morning arrived, cold and misting. Inside the dome, it was life as usual at a comfortable 72 degrees. It was bath day, and Uprights made their way to their routine appointments. Everyone knew the news of the escaped Upright, Jack, the captured Lura, and there was a raising of eyebrows and muffled whispers in the streets.

Gretchen crossed the lane, a few motorized wheelchairs out and about. She was five-eight, with round hips and a straight spine. She wore her hair in a ponytail, held with a tan rubber band. Her face was simple, pretty. At the dark brown cement residence, 5400, she scanned her ID and decided to work from the top floor down. She would have ten Infirm to bathe, roughly thirty minutes with each.

Her first Infirm of the day was Darla Doppel, an induced paraplegic with no kidneys and a colostomy tube. She had diabetes and suffered from aquagenic urticaria, an allergy to water, which was rare and highly prized. With her tall pile of white hair, she looked rather royal, although flabby and with thin lips as pale as butterfly blood.

Gretchen knocked and scanned herself in. Darla was in bed and calling to her before the door fully opened. "Well, hey, get in here. Earlier than usual, hey?"

"Hey there, Mrs. Doppel." Gretchen spoke with a thick southern accent. "Bath time." She glanced at the Chatty, tuned to the local news channel. The host, with multiple sclerosis, diabetes (a bright red monitor on her forehead flashed his blood sugar), and a heart that beat outside of his body, was querying a panel of experts, three with mechanical voice boxes, on the mauling of the judge, Chet Spurlock.

"Perhaps he suffers from a mental illness. We have to consider that," said a torso leaned back in his chair. He was bald with low-set ears. Mental illness was a specialty reserved for a select few of the Infirm. Usually, they were artists of some sort and ranked high.

"Yesss, he kid be crossin' oveer," said another without a lower jaw.

"But why did he attack the good judge?" said another, "Supposing that he's not mentally ill? Isn't it a bit late for that development?"

"Only the Great One would know the answer to that," said the host. He was dressed in a black t-shirt that covered his chest tube. He had a collapsed lung and wheezed when he spoke. "It's blasphemous regardless."

Gretchen gathered the supplies to bathe Darla. Due to Darla's water allergy, she would rub her body and hair with a special sweet-smelling powder.

"Ready, dear?" said Gretchen.

"Oh, I'm ready. Did you know this Jack? He sounds like a real beast."

"Never met him." Gretchen pulled off Darla's silky pants and top. Darla's big white breasts flopped to the sides. "You want your water first?" Darla was forced to have one glass of water per day to survive. She had a feeding tube protruding from a roll of fat on her belly. Otherwise, the water burned her mouth and throat.

"Yeah, go on and get it over with. Just don't spill none on me."

Gretchen drew water into a catheter-tipped syringe and plunged it into the feeding tube until the glass was empty. "You going out this afternoon?" said Gretchen. It was lunch day, too.

"I reckon so. I wish you could take me. It'll probably be some old guy I've never met before." Darla yawned.

"Well, I'm already hooked up, I'm afraid," said Gretchen. She checked the Scrumptious bin, and the can of liquid Scrumptious was there. "Got your breakfast here. Want that before your bath, sweetie?"

"Naw, let's get the bath done."

Darla started with her face and neck and worked her way down, rubbing the sandy powder onto her body with a cloth. She polished her arms, went up under her bosom, and continued down the line to her feet. "Okay, gonna turn you and get your back, sweetie." Gretchen heaved Darla onto her side and tackled her reddened back, the bedsheet catching the powder runoff. The only thing left was Darla's head, and Gretchen scrubbed and then combed out her pile of white hair, the air going a bit dusty. "There, babydoll, all done."

"You gonna empty my bag, dear?"

"Oh, yeah, gotta do that," said Gretchen. She grabbed the vacuum tube from the wall and inserted it into the colostomy bag filled with mousy liquid. The waste slurped away. Next, she pushed in the can of liquid Scrumptious. Darla made swallowing motions with her throat.

On the Chatty, the talk had turned to Jack's possible whereabouts, complete with a new panel of Infirm experts sharing their opinions. An aerial map showed the Netherlands west of the dome, noting water sources.

A plump and tender expert on the Netherlands spoke. His empty eye sockets oozed a thin serous fluid. "He most likely will have emerged from the sewer complex, as they are essentially dry. If he's lucky, he'll find water. Otherwise, he will have to return the dome to survive." He smacked his lips.

The host, whose heart could be seen beating beneath his silver shirt, wondered if Jack could make it to the next dome, Laramore, thirty-one miles west. There was some rivalry between the domes, and one panelist suggested that he could perhaps find asylum there, owing to their recent loss and humiliation in the Infirm Games. This sparked a lively debate, complete with insults about the people of Laramore. In the vote for election of the Great One, the dome of Laramore had gone with a young man whose torso had been joined to that of a deformed goat. Needless to say, the Great One was not prone to reward the people of Laramore with favors of any sort.

Gretchen turned away from the Chatty and looked around the small room, wondering if she was finished. "You want up in the chair, babydoll? I better get going."

"Thank you, dear," said Darla. "Put the cushion

in the chair, would you?"

Gretchen put the rubber eggcrate cushion into Darla's motorized wheelchair and brought it close to the bed. "Up we go." She pivoted Darla and landed her on the seat. She propped Darla's useless legs on the foot pedals. "There."

"Thank you, dear. And you be careful out there. There's no telling what might happen next."

"Will do," said Gretchen. She took a deep breath and exited, swiping her ID. Her next patient would be more challenging, a bitter old man who whistled when he wasn't blabbing.

Gretchen knocked and swiped her ID. She heard the whistling stop.

"That you? Get your pretty little bottom in her, girl." It was Danny Suggs. His bright, toothless smile greeted Gretchen. He had the top three: diabetes, heart disease, and cancer. He had just undergone treatment to extend the cancer from his brain to his genitals. He also had survived his two suicide attempts, which was a source of pride. He had hung by his neck for nearly five minutes on the last try. The record was eight.

"Watch your pretty mouth, big boy," said Gretchen. She sighed. The Chatty was on the porn channel, a naked Upright woman sliding a dildo in and out of an Infirm's eye socket. She looked away and nearly spit. "Can we change the channel, sweet, sweet boy?"

"You're the prude, are you? How about some nature?" He clicked the button on the back of his tooth, and the channel switched to a still picture of a gingko tree. The still enlarged, fuzzed, and then faded into a patch of green grass.

"That's much better, babydoll. Let's get this bath over and done." Darla drew up a pan of hot water with liquid soap. She undressed him and started with his pasty face.

"Get my ears now, darling. I couldn't pay you to take that top off, could I?"

Gretchen ignored him and dug into his ears with the washcloth, scooping out dead flesh and wax. "Lord." She rinsed the cloth and worked his flabby chest and arms.

"Say, sweet thing, you know anything about that crazy Upright, Jack something, the one that violated the judge?"

"See nothing, hear nothing," said Gretchen. "I've heard the judge is an ass."

"Better watch your tongue, young lady. I'll report you." He sighed as she bathed his special parts, a bit of gangrene already showing there on the tip of his member.

"You do that, big boy, and then you'll have some dude with long fingernails taking care of you." Darla turned him on his side and tackled his back. There was a deep sore over his tailbone, but he wanted it to grow, perhaps rot it out. Darla looked away and turned him back. "Okay, up in the chair, good buddy, and I'll make your bed."

Suggs could stand, a point of contention among his few friends, but could not walk due to his severed hamstrings. He dropped into the wheelchair with an *oomph.* He gazed at an image of the Great

One superimposed over a small green pond. He kissed the back of his hand in appreciation. "You're a good girl."

"And you're a bad boy." Gretchen laughed, wondering if her black tooth showed. It was due to be replaced. The Infirm liked their Uprights spic and span. "Okay, you're done. I'm sticking a fork in you."

The channel clicked back to porn, two young Upright girls, kissing each other's nipples.

"Okay, bye," said Gretchen. She swiped her ID and stepped into the hall. Eight more to go, and she wanted to pull her hair out. She wondered who would take Lura's patients and wished them luck. She would most certainly be executed on live Chatty.

~

The moon was rising, the temperature dropping. Jack walked, swinging his arms, making fists. He was thirsty again and longed for a brick of Scrumptious. Surely there would be some sort of food in the woods. He began to think he was walking in circles and decided he had to rest or risk passing out from exhaustion. He found a thick patch of pine straw and heaped it over his legs and then his chest. He lay there on his back, the ground hard, his stomach growling. He was just about to get comfortable when he had to pee. He cursed and stood. Soon he was back under the pine straw, gazing up through the gaps in the canopy at a sky bursting with stars. The sight amazed him, and he imagined that some warmth was to be had from them. He shivered and closed his eyes, begging the gods to let him sleep.

Perhaps ten minutes had passed, and the lumps beneath his shoulders were beginning to soften when he swore that he heard something. "What the!" He tried to stand but tripped and fell. A bright light shone into his eyes, and he winced. Sounds of feet in pine straw.

"Who are you?" said a voice, a regular voice.

"Okay, you got me. No need for questions. I'm Jack. I chopped off the judge's dick and balls. I admit it. Just get me a blanket and some food."

There was laughter from in front and behind. "Well, surprise, surprise. Jack. We've had our eyes out for you, friend."

"Friend?"

The flashlight lit up the speaker's face. A large face framed in rough-cut hair, with large, yellowed teeth. He was Bard. "You're safe with us, good buddy. My, my, what a catch."

Jack struggled to stand, shivering worse than ever. "Who are you?"

"Why, we're the Merry Woodsmen, good buddy. Never heard of us?"

"Only...rumors," said Jack. "I need a blanket, something hot. His breath made fog as he talked. I trust you, I guess. I thought you were from the dome. They're on my trail for sure."

"Baby, you got that right. But their flunkies will have to deal with us first, and they would rather avoid that. I'm Bard." Bard held out his gloved hand. "Behind you is Ismael."

"Well, hot damn, nice to meet you." Jack was shaking like a leaf in a hurricane. He shook Bard's hand and turned to shake Ismael's.

"Let's get you back to HQ, what do you say? Follow us. Cut off a judge's balls! I like you already."

"Sounds...good. How far?" said Jack. He gazed at Ismael. He was thin and brown with a stringy goatee and carried what looked to be a rifle. He'd read about them in the library.

"Not far, the walk will warm you up. But no more flashlight. Let the moon do its work." Bard set off at a brisk clip, followed by Jack and then Ismael. Off-trail, they walked the rolling hills for another twenty minutes before coming to a cliff face. "Okay, just walk on the rocks till we get to the cave. Got it?"

Barely able to contain his shivering, Jack stumbled from one rock to the next. He fell and cursed.

Bard helped him up, and Ismael ruffled the ground where he had fallen. The cliff face rose twelve feet or so. Bard disappeared into a narrow cleft. Jack turned sideways and followed for a good thirty feet. He could feel openness around him and stopped, listening to the breath of the other two. Bard lit a candle on a rock, and weak light seeped into the room. Jack's eyes adjusted, and he could discern a fire ring, a stack of wood, and two crude pallets.

"What's next?" said Jack. "I need a blanket before I shake myself to death."

"Yeah," said Bard, "and some hot coffee. Ismael, grab that blanket off my bed."

Ismael did so, and Jack sat on a smooth stone with the blanket wrapped around him. Bard poked at the coals in the fire ring, bringing up a small flame. He added wood, and a fire soon licked the shadows. Ismael poured water into a large can, added some used coffee grounds, and set it into the fire.

"Cut his balls off, did you? And his pecker too?" said Bard.

Jack's teeth chattered. "I had to. He had it coming. Told me to lick him there, and I refused. I'd had plenty of him on sex day. The bastard."

"Good Lord. Sex day. It's a wonder you poor Uprights take it. Why is that? Not me, though, good buddy."

Jack looked from one face to the other. "Well, it's the way we're raised, right? To take it from the damned Infirm. God, every time I see the Great One's big watermelon head, I want to stick it with a knife."

"We've not seen the new one," said Ismael. He warmed his hands over the fire.

"Yeah, we move around," said Bard. "No Chatties out here."

"I could live with that," said Jack. He let the blanket relax and smoothed back his brown hair. "So, is it safe here?"

"Well, safe for now. The Infirm are afraid of the dark. They won't even send their lackeys out at night. But come morning, they'll be looking, most likely with the helicopter. Pussies, and I should know. Ismael and I used to be part of Squad. One day, we just didn't go back. How do you like them taters?" Bard laughed, filling the room with sound.

"I was wondering," said Jack. He pressed his hands against his neck, feeling the pulse there. "So, what? Now I'm one of you guys?"

"Indeed, you are," said Ismael. "No turning back now. You'll be executed, probably on the spot, and taped, of course, for the Infirm to enjoy."

"Yep, the Merry Woodsmen. You, me, and Ismael. How do you like them taters?" Bard laughed again.

"Do you just hide and run? I mean that could get old pretty quick."

"We have plans. Don't make it sound so dire. There's lots for us to do," said Bard. "We took out the power supply at Laramore for a full hour about four months ago. That really shook 'em up."

"Well, that's something," said Jack. "I did a bad thing and got another Upright tangled up in this mess, a woman. I'm sure they've caught her. I have to do something to help her out, rescue her before the ax falls. Could we do it?" He then explained how he'd stumbled into her room, how she was high on Champy, and that he'd basically abducted her.

Bard cracked his knuckles. "Well, we heard about her, too. That would be mighty tricky, a rescue, but not impossible."

"How did you hear this? You don't have a Chatty."

"Radio," said Ismael. "We get all the chatter, especially from Squad." He pointed to a backpack with an antenna sticking out.

"Have to watch that battery, though," said Bard. "Once a day. That's it."

The water in the can was boiling, and Ismael lifted it from the fire with a rag. "Coffee, to warm you up?"

"What's coffee?" said Jack.

"A drink," said Bard. "Go on. You'll like it. We get it from the wama, abandoned. Might be bitter."

Jack took a steaming metal cup from Ismael. He smelled the brew. "Smells good." He sipped and made a face. "Good Lord, that is bitter."

"Warm, though, right?" said Bard.

"Yeah, much appreciated," said Jack, and he sipped again, spitting out coffee grounds. "God, I just want to sleep."

"Got some extra plastic, is all. You can cover up with that," said Bard. He carefully dipped a cup of coffee. "But, first, you gotta tell us more about the judge, what you did. Sounds a little over the top to me, but you don't look crazy."

Jack looked grim, not sure that he'd actually done it. He relayed the story quickly.

Ismael grunted and shook his head.

Bard just grinned. "Look, it's nearly midnight. We'll take care of the watches tonight, but you'll join in tomorrow. Go ahead and get some rest. I'd offer you food, but we're plumb out. We was headed to the wama when we found you."

"Yeah, I'm starved, but I can wait. I appreciate you taking me in, putting yourselves in more danger." He took a big drink of coffee and coughed, and soon he was ready to call it a night with Ismael watching from the entrance and Bard beneath his blanket. Jack rolled himself up in the plastic and closed his eyes, his mind racing, his heart thudding.

~

Gretchen's last patient of the day at 5400 were conjoined twins, attached at the back of the head. They had the largest suite on the first floor with a tiny window. They'd had their legs removed, but were otherwise mobile, scooting around on their stumps like two crabs, staring at the ceiling with bug eyes. Finished, Gretchen stepped outside. She wanted a cigarette bad, but there was only one place in the city she could smoke, and that was only on Saturday. She looked up to the dome where the time was superimposed with a laser. Two o'clock. Her next task was to take an Infirm out to one of the numerous small clubs around town for a bite to eat and socializing with other Infirm. Her regular was an old man of seventy with massive tumors bulging from his body. His head was a regular mess, his nose on the side of his face, his mouth just a pucker hidden beneath a wad of purply flesh. He'd chosen to be paralyzed by gunshot, a romantic notion from days gone by.

Gretchen walked up two blocks, passed a gathering of Infirm and their Uprights, and headed to 6767. Mr. Grub was on the second floor, and she knocked and swiped her ID. Delmar Grub sat in his wheelchair holding the giant tumor that grew on his chest. He garbled out a few words. He was freshly bathed, and his thin gray hair combed straight back over the bumps on his scalp.

"I got your number, Mr. Grub," said Gretchen. She didn't necessarily dislike Delmar and might as well have as much fun as she could. She patted him on the shoulder. He wore a stretchy gold shirt, a pair of loose shorts, and house shoes. "Ready?"

Delmar mumbled and squeaked. On the Chatty was an update regarding Jack and the mutilated judge. Squad had failed to find him, and he was assumed to be wandering the Netherlands. The current panel of experts believed that he'd soon be caught. The screen switched to an image of the judge, holding forth in his courtroom, his face red and strained. As a result of the attack, his status was being further elevated to supreme. Who knew? Maybe one day he'd take over as the Great One and would have Jack to thank. But very few Great Ones came from the South.

To get through the door, Gretchen had to adjust the giant chest tumor and soon was down the ramp and onto the street. "Where to, big fella? The usual?"

Delmar grunted his approval, and they headed to the Happy Pilgrim. There was a small crowd already there, sitting at café tables outside, and shouts of Delmar! came. He waved at the friendly faces and drooled onto his shirt. Gretchen pulled him up to a table with two older women who had no teeth. Both wore lipstick and too much eye shadow. One, Ophelia, was hunched over with severe scoliosis, her nose touching the tablecloth. The other, Mayrene, succumbed to routine drownings and looked kind of like a fish. They said their hellos and made small talk with Delmar. He grunted and slurped.

Gretchen went inside and ordered a chocolate milkshake for Delmar, along with a bowl of applesauce, his favorite. He liked to drink whiskey, but drinking day was Thursday, and he would be with another Upright. For herself, she ordered a glass of water and a cube of Scrumptious, all that she was allowed. The small café had a few tables inside and was decorated with small red barn doors on the walls, one of which said "See Rock City." The fellow who ran the Happy Pilgrim was Homer, and he whispered to Gretchen. "What do you know?"

Gretchen knew he was referring to the mutilation. She glanced at the cameras in every corner and just shrugged. "Nothing." She waited.

"Gonna be trouble." He made big eyes.

"Good," said Gretchen. She took a mint from the bowl and headed back to Delmar, nodding to the other Uprights there. She sat down.

"Gonna string him up good," said Ophelia. She was having the pureed lamb stew. Her Upright, known just as 52, pulled it into a syringe and flushed the brown liquid into her mouth. She swallowed with flair.

"Serve him right," said Mayrene.

Gretchen watched the other Upright, a handsome fellow named Norman, inject a pureed Waldorf salad into Mayrene's feeding tube. Within minutes, it would be spurting into her colostomy bag. Gretchen made eye contact with Norman and could tell he knew something. He was making the face tic for "shower" and spelled out Jack in rapid sign language.

Nothing was lost on 52, and he nodded. Between squirts of lamb stew, salad, and slurps of milkshake, the three Uprights carried on a covert, lively conversation. Gretchen learned that Norman had taken showers with Jack. The supposition among the Upright was that the judge was a royal prick and deserved his fate, although they were chagrined that he would be elevated as a result. Talk among the Infirm turned to sex day, and Mayrene and Ophelia brightened.

"I don't need it so much anymore," said Mayrene. Her mouth formed an O when she wasn't talking. "But I got randy and had that girl give me a good old-fashioned carpet cleaning." She laughed, a twinkle in her eye.

Ophelia tried to lift her head a bit. "Had me a man. I just let him do what comes natural. I'm getting too old, though. I'll need artificial parts sooner than later." She sighed.

Delmar grunted and drooled, talking, but no one listening. He opened his mouth for a bite of applesauce, holding back the tumor dropping from his jaw.

Gretchen also learned that word was out that the Merry Woodsmen were in radio contact with the underground, a handful of disenchanted Squad who had access to communications. The Infirm were in charge, but their fascination with disability made them vulnerable. Without the services of the Upright, everything would just go to hell. Gretchen signed that her ears were to the ground and felt a tingle of excitement that something improbable was in the works.

~

Since the mutilation that morning, Central was

in high gear. There would be tele-visits from the higher-ups in Washington, no doubt. With their Uprights in tow, a plan had been formed, a reward to be offered, the opportunity to become an Infirm for those with information that led to the capture of Jack.

The five men and six women who made up Central lived together in a low, maroon building marked with a flashing C, always accompanied by their personal Uprights. Cornelius Fava, the head of Central, was black as shoe polish, a quadriplegic with permanent torticollis that pulled his large head to the right, just like the Great One. The members of Central rarely met in person, relying on videoconferencing, the controls embedded behind their false teeth. They were gathered on their video screens, which they wore on their heads, simulating a conference room.

"Well, it's best to take him alive," said Cornelius. "He'll have information on his accomplices, including this Lura character." His voice was smooth and inflected.

"Agreed," said Thelma Butts. "This has the makings of a conspiracy. It's no accident she was with him." Thelma, a paraplegic, suffered from hyperhidrosis, extreme sweating, and she kept a small towel inside her video hat.

"But her record is clean as a pin," said Cornelius. "She says that he abducted her, that she was under the influence of Champy." *Influence* coming long and slow with four syllables. "Why would he need someone who Champy temporarily disabled?"

Leroy Smalls spoke. His eyes had been removed. "The perfect alibi, if you ask me. Kidnapped my ass." Stomach cancer was eating away his insides, and he coughed blood into his video hat. His Upright intervened with a tissue.

"Hmm, well, maybe so, but I'm not convinced. You know who the judge will be who tries her? Chet Spurlock himself, once he's recovered, and he'll have her hide, guilty or no."

"More power to him."

"Amen."

"Well," said Cornelius, "she must surely pay, but we need to see the bigger picture here." He cleared his throat. Heads nodded.

"So, what's the plan?" said Thelma. "What's next?"

Cornelius paused, then spoke. "I think we are agreed that a vigorous interrogation of our prisoner is in order. We'll want to interview her patients as well for incriminating information. As soon as day breaks, we have Squad headed into the Netherlands, as well as helicopter surveillance. I predict he'll give up, missing the comforts of home, least of which are food and water. Mr. Smalls, perhaps you would privy us to the information you have thus far gathered on this Lura."

Smalls' eye slits quivered. "Her parents gave her up, separated out, and declared Upright twenty-seven years ago. Her parents, upstanding Infirm converted from Uprights over ten years ago. They died of peritonitis after her large intestine was piggybacked onto his rectum. There was a story about them in the *Digest,* you might recall." He paused and ran a finger across his gummy eye slits. "She was raised in the orphanage, kept healthy, and excelled at the game known as volleyball. She never incurred any demerits and was rumored to have won an underground beauty pageant. She is striking, if I might add. She entered service at the age of sixteen, having done well in her health courses. That's about it."

"Thank you, Mr. Smalls." Cornelius clicked his tongue. He imagined that his foot was itching, but there was nothing he could do about it. He motioned for his Upright to give him a sip of water. "Well, that's enough on Lura. What about this Jack fellow, Peters?"

"Yes, my pleasure." Peter Peters was a dwarfish man blessed with soft bones, osteomalacia. He'd had an even 100 broken of his 206 bones, but could still manage to stand with help, usually showing off at a party. "Where to begin? I suppose all of the warning signs were there to begin with. I daresay our system is far too lenient with the likes of him. He was forcibly removed from his parents, themselves Uprights, and grew up in the city of Parched Lips, just a skip and a jump from the state line with Tennessee. Records are sketchy from there, but it seems he routinely disrespected his Infirm wards and was once disciplined for giving a hot-water enema. He excelled in his health courses there, but was transferred here at the age of eighteen, the reasons being unclear, other than we needed more Uprights to care for the Infirm. He's now thirty-one years of age and in his service has been demoted on three occasions, all for disrespecting his superiors. He's been known to disable a Chatty here and there, which should have been a clear warning. He's, to say the least, obstreperous, even bumptious, and now highly dangerous. He's done gone and taken liberties with the life of one of our own, the good Judge Spurlock."

A variety of *hmms, hahs,* and *huhs* parried back and forth.

"A real devil," said Butts.

"It seems," said Cornelius. "Well, let us adjourn for now. I know that most of you are hankering to be out and about. It is lunch day after all, and I'm just about desiccated thinking about an ice cream float." He laughed, and the others laughed as well. Plus, he was craving a cigar.

~

Having spent the night in isolation, Lura was moved into a cell with another Upright, Mae, who was in for attempting suicide (a no-no for Uprights), a failed hanging on bath day right in front of a bed-bound Infirm. Mae was short and prim with large red lips and a winsome smile, which she flashed even when she was sad.

Being the newcomer, Lura took the top bunk. Since her health classes had ended, she'd not been in the same small room with another Upright, and she found it difficult to talk. Mae was curious, though, and prodded her for information about the mutilation of the judge, but Lura had nothing much to say, only recounting being toted through the streets and the park by Jack.

"I was too high to go in the sewer," she said.

"That's what I miss most, the Champy. They don't give you jack squat in this miserable place. Have to beg for it." Mae paced around the small cell, touching the wall and bunks as she went.

That was of interest to Lura. "No Champy. That's gonna suck. How are we supposed to sleep?"

"Ask somebody who knows," said Mae. "Say, would you like to have sex? The guards don't mind. They like to watch. I hate fucking with the Infirm, but I'm horny as hell most of the time. You've got a pretty face."

"Well, no," said Lura. Her heart beat a little faster. She'd never had sex with an Upright. "I guess I prefer men." She thought about Jack with his wide shoulders, his brown hair, his humble nature.

"Well, it don't hurt to ask, do it?" said Mae. She flushed the toilet just to hear it and watched the water swirl away. "You got a thing for this Jack? I bet you do. I can hear it in your voice. I bet you'd like to suck him off. Am I right? Especially after he gave what-for to the damn judge. God, that's precious. Stuffed his balls into his mouth. Talk about a mouthful." Mae cackled.

"I only knew him from the showers and the library. He's not bad-looking. Seems like a real nice guy. I can't imagine him doing such a thing, although..."

"That damn judge had it coming to him. He's the one who put me in here. Next time I'll find a rope instead of a sheet." She explained to Lura why she was in.

Lura had often contemplated killing herself, the never-ending grind of serving the Infirm. It seemed like the only way out, other than becoming one of them, which she had sworn she would never do. Once a year, on December 25th, five Uprights were allowed to become Infirm, and most took it.

There was a whoosh and a clink. The Scrumptious had arrived, and Mae was first there. "Only sent one brick. Must not have you on the list." She took the brick, leaving Lura to fend for herself. "I'd offer you a bite, but I'm plumb starved. I hate this shit." She chewed and drew down a plastic cup of water. "Catch that guard when he comes by."

Lura went to the bars, staring through them at a blank wall with a silent Chatty every ten feet or so. *Murder, on trains, is to be expected. When preparing ape, discard the feet and hands.* She gazed at the close-up of the Great One. She could see little hairs in his nose. Voices echoed from up and down the hall. She wondered about her fate, or was it bad luck, getting tangled with the very man she thought she had a crush on. She had been able to tell that he was a wildcard, a mischievous look in his brown eyes, or were they green? The guard was approaching, his stun gun at his side.

"Hey, guard?"

"What you need?" The guard was Upright but had sworn an oath of loyalty to serve and protect the Infirm. His name was Teddy, and he enjoyed his life, not having to give baths to the nasty creatures. He wore the gray uniform with black boots, looking smart from head to toe.

"Some food. Mine didn't come."

"Huh, maybe they want to starve you a bit. Taking on that judge was a foolish idea if you ask me," said Teddy. His slicked-back hair exposed his shining temples.

"I never touched him," said Lura.

"Really? Not what I heard. I heard you did the stuffing." Teddy almost laughed.

"I was kidnapped, for God's sake. I'm the second victim here. The cameras will prove it. I wasn't there."

"Well," and Teddy tapped his stun gun, "I'd say you're in hot water, sister. I'll check on din-din for you, but it may cost you, if you know what I mean." He grinned.

"Yeah, whatever," said Lura. She felt a heat rising in her chest. "You're one of us. Don't forget it." Already, she was feeling like a hardened criminal.

"But I'm here, and you're there. Don't forget that." He mumbled into his radio, requesting Scrumptious for Lura, and moved on, headed to the heavy door and the next hallway.

"Shit," said Lura.

"Yeah, you'll learn quick, missy," said Mae. "Nothing comes cheap in here."

Lura felt a little sick and sat on the metal toilet, which didn't have a seat. "Any of these guards with us? I mean, they're like us. You'd think they'd sympathize."

"Hell," said Mae. "With the privileges they get? The free sex and smoking privileges seven days a week. I think not. But you never know, though. You got a plan?"

"I just got here. You're not a convert, are you?" said Lura. "Any special privileges?"

"Ha! You'd think I'd killed one of 'em. The last thing they want, though, is a dead Upright unless it's you. Unbalances everything, present company excluded. But I'd say they think you're low risk, putting you here and not in lockdown. You don't wanna go there. Drive you insane, from what I hear."

"What's it like?" said Lura. Her butt hurt from sitting on the hard toilet.

"Just isolation in a dark closet is the best I can tell. They have a fight day. Special channel on the Chatty. The winner gets half time in return."

"Ugh, fight day. That sounds horrible.

"Well, it's just the men with the men and the women with the women, so it could be worse."

There was a whoosh and a plunk, and Lura jumped up expecting a fight with Mae. She grabbed the Scrumptious and crawled to her top bunk, lay on her back, and chewed.

~

During the night, Bard and Ismael had rotated watch every two hours, without seeing anything other than a few raccoons. Early on, before they'd discovered the wama, they'd resorted to eating a few.

Jack opened his eyes, smelling smoke. A dull wash of light entered the cave. He had slept, but in fits, the plastic making him sweat. Bard was tending the fire, with Ismael entrenched at the entrance, keeping vigil. Jack was starving.

"Time to get on up, boy," said Bard. He was stirring a pot of oatmeal.

"Oh God, my back," said Jack. He unrolled himself and stood, stretching and groaning.

"Welcome to the woods," said Bard. He laughed. "We got to eat and get out of here. Squad's bound to be looking for us. Make our way right up close to the dome at Laramore. They got some tunnels, some caves, good hiding. I expect Squad thinks you'll just walk in circles and give up when they find you."

"If I give up, they'll kill me," said Jack.

"Damn straight," said Bard. "And us too, although they seem to have forgotten us, think we been eaten by bears, no doubt."

"Bears? Are they real?"

"Oh, yeah. In these parts, for sure. They mind their own business, eating berries and such, but we seen 'em more than once." He took the oatmeal from the fire to let it cool. "Got some old-fashioned Scrumptious here, called oatmeal. Real filling." He licked the wooden spoon.

With the light, Jack surveyed the long room with its tall ceiling that reached into darkness. There was graffiti. Leaning against the wall was a rucksack with supplies. He gazed at Bard, a big man, his old Squad uniform supplemented with a black jacket made of leather. His boots were scuffed and worn.

"Roll that plastic, boy, and hide it." Bard pointed up into the darkness. "There's a rock shelf. Press yourself in the crack and climb up."

Jack leaned back and eyed the crack. He did as he was told and was within reach of the shelf. He reached down for the plastic held out by Bard. Just then, Ismael returned.

"The helicopter," said Ismael. "They're looking." He had painted his face with soot from the fire and looked a little wild with his goatee, kind of like a cannibal.

"Hurry, boy," said Bard. "The Squad's out on foot, no doubt as well. We got some tough humping to do." He braced the rucksack and hefted it to his shoulders.

Jack slid down, feeling his synthetic shirt grind against the rock. He realized that he could very well be caught, that his night of rest could just be the beginning of a long struggle. "Shit. What do we do?"

Ismael cradled the rifle. "We walk, that's what, and run like hell if needed." His Squad uniform was in worse shape than Bard's, a big rip over his calf, but his boots looked pretty new.

Jack looked down at his standard issue Upright shoes, flimsy things not made for walking on dirt and rocks. "I'm ready when you are."

"Here, wolf this down," said Bard. He spooned in a mouthful of oatmeal and passed the pot to Ismael. Ismael passed it to Jack. The oatmeal was flat and gummy. Soon, the pot was empty, but Jack felt a spark of energy.

Bard led the way, followed by Jack. "You stay in the middle, boy. Got it? If I say duck, duck. If I say run, run."

Jack nodded and stepped into the light, amazed

at the trees, mostly pine with a few hardwoods: oaks, maples, no gingkoes. He felt alive as they stepped away from the rock face and made their way into a ravine, then headed straight up, leaning into the ground. Not used to such activity, right away, Jack's heart rate jumped, and he could feel the blood pumping in his neck. Up they went for nearly half a mile before cresting a small ridge without a view. On they walked, away from Pan and toward Laramore with a stop at the wama along the way.

The helicopter had faded, but now it came to them again, a beating of the air. Bard motioned, and they hunkered down beneath a stand of rhododendron. Jack had warmed with all of the exercise, but chilled whenever they stopped. After five minutes, the chopper noise diminished.

The terrain was rolling, up and down, and they skirted downed trees and piles of dead limbs. At every sight of birds, usually small wood sparrows, Jack marveled and tried not to think of his aching ankles. They stopped, and Ismael took the pack from Bard, Bard taking the rifle, a .22 with six rounds.

Two hours passed, and all in a sweat, they followed a ridge and plunged into another ravine where a creek flowed over roots and smooth stones. They stopped and drank with their hands. Jack was exhausted.

"What you think, boy?" said Bard. "Next is your turn to take the pack."

"Well, I feel the gravity. I'm not used to hills, just flat surfaces." Jack wiped sweat from his eyes.

"Yep, hill country, no doubt, but we'll soon come

to a flat place, used to be a city, small one, but with this big warehouse. Haven't been in a couple of months. Need to stock up. Get you some new boots. It's like you done died and gone to heaven."

"Food there?" said Jack.

Ismael grunted. "Yeah, like you've never seen before, in cans and packages. A lot of it's spoiled, but there's plenty for years to come."

The trees began to thin, and the ground leveled, but the underbrush thickened, and they plowed through it, leaving a marked trail of their progress. Soon, they were crossing old foundations and what were once roads, still with leaning rusted signs that said Stop and Yield. Tall poles with ragged wires. On they walked, having been underway for four hours or more. And there it was, a vast clearing, junk trees and weeds growing in cracks of what was once a large parking lot. Jack looked at the large building just ahead and read the sign, Wa- Ma--. The wama, as they called it.

"Now we run," said Bard, "straight to those doors. The glass is busted. Ready?" Without waiting, he broke into a trot.

With the rucksack weighing him down and his ankles and feet screaming, Jack bolted after him with Ismael on his tail.

Into the wama they went, the bright light diminished, and all was quiet.

"What you think?" said Bard.

Jack looked around. There were little stations with odd-looking machines. The floor was littered with cardboard and dust. The ceiling was high, perhaps twenty feet, and pipes and ductwork snaked along there. Beyond were aisles of clothing and food. "Well, I'll be darned," said Jack. He turned and read a sign, "Subway."

"Ismael, you see if you can find another rucksack and load it with food. I'll get Jack here a coat and some shoes."

Ismael nodded and headed off to the outdoor gear.

Jack followed Bard, walking between shelves of what looked to be notebooks, pens, folders, and all sorts of things hanging on racks. They passed a grimed glass case, and Jack peered in. Watches. "Hey, can I get one? I think I broke mine."

"Don't work, batteries all dead," said Bard. "Keep your mind on the job, boy."

They walked through an area filled with circular racks of women's clothing and came to several aisles of shoes. Bard walked him up to a section of boots. "Try some on. You need 'em."

"Right," said Jack. "But there's only one of each."

"Look in the boxes, boy. Them are just for show."

Jack found a pair of leather boots with what looked to be a gum sole. He sat on the floor and pulled off his simple cloth shoes. "They got socks?"

"Yeah, they got socks. I'll grab you a pair. Hurry. We ain't got all day."

Jack tried to pull on the boot, but it was too small. He grabbed another box. Too small. Bard returned and threw a pair of brown socks in the floor.

"Thanks," said Jack.

"Oh, hell, the helicopter," said Bard. "Hurry!"

Jack grabbed a random box, and it was a different boot, black and cushy. He slid it on. It was a bit too big, and he pulled it off and slipped on the socks. The helicopter. He pulled on one boot, and then the other.

"Shit, we got to get out of here, boy. Let's go. Out the back way."

Jack was trying to tie the laces and felt Bard jerk him by the shoulder. "Tie 'em later. Go!"

Jack stood and stumbled after Bard. The helicopter had landed in the parking lot, the engine whining. Through aisles of everything one could imagine, Jack trotted after Bard. He tripped over his laces, bent down, and stuffed them into the boots. They passed what Jack recognized as Chatties and passed through swinging doors into a dark, open room. In the back was a square of light, and they ran for it.

~

With Delmar Grubb and his tumors back to 6767, Gretchen had two hours before shower time. There was not much to do, other than visit the museum, which she had memorized, but it was a chance to brush against other Uprights, whisper a few words, and feel somewhat normal.

In bright red letters, the sign simply said "Disability," and she scanned herself inside the clean, airy building. A frail woman in a wheelchair with a homunculus on the side of her head smiled and, with a mechanical claw, offered her a bottle of flavored water, a treat, and Gretchen took the cold bottle, lemon. On the label was a photo of the patron saint of the Infirm, a strange character named Jerry Lewis, who had helped make muscular dystrophy all the rage back in the old days. The small anteroom, bright yellow and circular, branched off in three directions to hallways highlighting diseases and infirmities, disability equipment, and medical technology, all in chronological order. The museum was not comprehensive, being of local flavor. The real deal was in Washington, D.C.

To the soothing music of violins, Gretchen entered the hall of diseases and infirmities, a shadowy lane with exhibits on either side. She noticed two other Uprights, a man and a woman, standing close to one another but apart, using subtle sign language, a love affair no doubt being played out in one of the few places where such a thing could occur. The first station paid homage to diabetes, one of those long-suffering diseases with an endless array of complications that generated billions of healthcare dollars. The wall plaque noted the popularity of diabetes, estimating that over ninety percent of the Infirm were afflicted, making it the most requested mutation. Those who developed insulin-dependent diabetes naturally as adolescents were deemed especially lucky and attained a higher rank than those modified.

Gretchen moved on, half paying attention to the exhibits and half to the man and woman who seemed to be orbiting one another without making eye contact. The next exhibit, complete with a projected image of a stomach, was dedicated to stomach cancer, a regional specialty in the South. Intestinal cancers were frowned on, making the absorption of nutrients difficult, but stomach cancer was all the rage. The text praised the disease as vigorous, robust, and painful, requiring multiple surgeries and pain medications, a boon to local economies. Cancer cells, it was explained, had the best interest of the Infirm at heart, a "mutual friend." Gretchen looked through the oversized microscope at a slide of a stomach cancer cell, large whitish cells among pink and purple healthy cells.

The music droned on, and Gretchen crossed the hall and stood in front of a popular infirmity, spina bifida. Many were born with it, but medical technology had made it possible to extract the spine and carry it in a sack on one's lap. Of course, naturally occurring spina bifida was seen as an omen of great fortune. The display of a spinal cord in a vat of goo made Gretchen sick to her stomach, and she turned away. The man was cupping his fingers, basically having virtual sex with the woman, who appeared to be near orgasm by the look on her face. Gretchen could only smile, wishing for such a relationship herself. She had been following the mutilation of the judge on the Chatty and had found the frequent images of Jack alluring and had begun imagining him as a great hero or perhaps a lover. She pinched herself and moved on.

Next was a rather humdrum display that highlighted the subtle but toxic effects of high blood pressure. Those with the disorder were seen as mundane, as there was little visually to appreciate.

The disease was most noted for causing strokes, which did cause paralysis if left untreated. The droopy smiles and slurred speech of those with hemorrhagic strokes were seen as good luck. There was a machine to check one's blood pressure, which registered the numbers in five-foot letters. Gretchen knew her blood pressure was normal, but put her arm in the gadget, nonetheless. It pumped and squeezed her arm. The bright display blinked and then threw onto the wall: 110/60. An image of a sad face appeared below. Gretchen sighed and walked casually from one display to the next, keeping her eye on the time for her daily shower. Missing shower was punishable by ten lashes. Punishment day was every day.

Gretchen lost the couple and saw only two others, both women, both alone. She sipped the last of her lemon drink and came to the final exhibit, the almighty disorder, muscular dystrophy, which had started it all, which had led the country down its path of disability bliss. A video clip of a live telethon played, Jerry Lewis extolling viewers to call in and donate. Beside him was a shriveled man in a wheelchair, suffering from a severe loss of muscle mass and paralysis. A machine breathed for him, and the look in his eyes was one of boredom and extreme suffering. He was known as Mickey among the Infirm and was popular on t-shirts and birthday cakes. Gretchen yawned and checked her watch, only fifteen minutes till shower, and she exited the display hall, nodded to the old lady, and stepped onto the wide street. A scooter beeped, and she bristled.

The shower was only three blocks west, and she made it just in time, stepping into line, recognizing most of the faces. She dreaded seeing them naked, but moved inside to the disrobing room and waited her turn. She stepped into the cagelike contraption, like a stretcher frame, and leaned back. The whole thing was on rails and moved forward slowly, clanking, passing through a plastic flap into the bright shower room filled with steam. Naked, she shivered and glanced at the men on either side of her, both glancing at her with suggestive but grim smiles.

The water hit her, she closed her eyes, and then a mist of cleansing solution. It felt slippery and coated her body. The conveyor belt clanked, and she moved sideways, soon entering the rinse cycle. The whole process took exactly three minutes, and the machine delivered her to the drip room, where she relaxed for a moment before entering the chaos of drying from large nozzles of warm, jetted air. At the end, a beeper beeped, and she stepped out, pulling a towel from a moving belt to dry her hair. She then entered the dressing room, which she hated, being ogled by men and women, and received a clean blue uniform for the next day, which she would sleep in that night. On the way out, played a children's tune with a chorus of "Happy, happy, happy! Clean, clean, clean!" There was now nothing to do but return to her flat, and she did.

~

At Pan General Hospital, the disfigured judge, Chet Spurlock, lay in bed, griping about the coarseness of the sheets. At home, his were silk. He occupied one of the large private rooms at the end of the hall. His genital wounds had been sutured, but he was awaiting a prosthetic penis and artificial testicles, which would be attached by robot, guided by a specialist in Maryland. The judge's nurse, Marilyn, knocked on the door. She was tall and pretty with curly blonde hair, her chin and cheekbones prominent.

"Come in, for god's sake," said the judge. "And where's my anal beads?" Every day was sex day in the hospital.

Marilyn flinched at the harshness of his voice. "I've ordered them. They have to come from central supply."

"Well, at least pleasure me. It's not like I'm contagious." He snapped his fingers, and his lazy eye roved the room. He was squat and dumpy with hunched shoulders and thin white hair that looked like thread.

"Well," said Marilyn, "dialysis is in thirty minutes. We have to think about that."

"Don't try and flatter me. You know you want me, girl." He slapped his hands together. "Just a little taste is all I need, just a finger or two."

Marilyn hated to do it to Debbie. "Okay, let me get the nursing assistant, Debbie Dee." Everyone called her Debbie Dee.

"No, I want you! Debbie Dee has cold sores. If there's one thing I won't tolerate, it's herpes. I don't care how common it is. Now get over here and do as I say."

"Okay," said Marilyn, her chest flushing red, "but I'm wearing gloves."

"Whatever, and take your top off. I like your tits."

Marilyn stiffened and ignored him. She popped on gloves. "Turn on your side. You know this could rip your stitches."

"Who cares? I'm getting a whole new package tomorrow. And I said, 'Take off your top.' I want a good look before I turn over."

Knowing she could lose her job, Marilyn pulled up her top above her breasts, which held there. "Got an eyeful?"

"Man, them are some knockers. I want you to be my personal nurse when I get out of here."

"Okay, turn over, sir." Marilyn put her hands on her hips.

"Whatever," and he turned on his side, grimacing at the stitches pulling.

Marilyn pulled the sheet down and slid his gown aside. Moles and black hairs covered the judge's back, his skin pasty and white. His butt seemed to be grinning at her, and she lifted a cheek. There was a cup of ice water on the overbed tray, and she dipped her thumb. She found his anus, rimmed with skin tags, and forced in her thumb.

"God dammit! Be careful, girl. Nice and easy, in and out. Ow, yeah, that's it. In and out, in and out."

Marilyn closed her eyes, imagining her day off, what she would do. She would walk to the park and sit beneath a gingko tree, perhaps run into her girlfriend, another nurse on the unit. She withdrew her thumb and went in with four fingers, ramming them in.

"Uh!" said the judge. "Harder."

Marilyn's girlfriend could make her come with her dense and rhythmic words. She focused on composing a verse, searching for a fresh scheme to describe her love and appreciation for her one true friend. She looked down, remembered what she was doing, and retched.

There was a knock on the door. "Dialysis," and a male nurse entered with a wheelchair.

Marilyn retrieved her disembodied fingers and pulled the gown down. "Dialysis, sir, is here for you." She hoped he would bleed to death on the machine.

"Well, damn," said the judge. "Hello, Randy." He knew everybody in dialysis.

Randy helped the judge sit up and transitioned him to the wheelchair. The judge could still walk with help, which was embarrassing, but he secretly feared becoming entirely reliant on the Upright.

Randy was giving Marilyn a look, and she realized her breasts were still exposed. She coughed, pulled her top down, and watched the judge disappear into the hall.

"Well, Randy, how's it hanging?" said the judge.

"Just fine, Mr. Spurlock." Randy took long strides when he walked. He was a bit overweight and kept his head shaved.

"Well, boy, it's Judge Spurlock. Lost your manners?"

"Sorry, sir. Judge Spurlock." He hit the elevator button for down.

Dialysis was on two, and the doors opened. "Cat

got your tongue, boy?" said the judge.

"Uh, yessir," said Randy. "There's a big old cat running around with my tongue." He grinned, looking down on the judge's thinning mop of white hair.

"Sounds like you're being a smartass, boy. I don't like it."

Randy kept quiet, passed radiology, and went through double doors into dialysis. A bank of ten dialysis machines lined the room, four with Infirm already hooked up. Two nurses sat at a small station, charting. The Infirm all looked sad and grumpy, the two with working digestive tracts munching candy. The impurities would be removed during dialysis.

Randy sidled the judge up to an empty reclining chair and helped him in. He would enjoy sticking the huge needle into the judge's shunt, which pulsed on his left arm. With the tubing cleared of air and filling with blood, Randy initiated the machine. "Good to go, sir, three hours today."

"Humph," said the judge. His eyes drifted to the Chatty, a nature show about a canyon where lived glowworms, not far away, it seemed. He liked that sort of thing and tried to relax, the dialysis machine humming at his side. "Get me some of that candy, boy," and Randy did, pocketing a piece for himself.

There was a murmur of conversation among the other patients, and then one moaned, a woman named Thelma Tompkins. She weighed 405 pounds. Her nurse jumped up and came over. Thelma's blood pressure had dropped to 80 over 40, and her heart rate had jumped to 140.

"Well, fudge," said the nurse. "Thelma? Thelma!" She hit the pause button on the machine, leaned Thelma back as far as the chair would go, then hit the code button. Thelma had stopped breathing. The nurse checked her watch. She was to wait five minutes to allow brain death to occur before attempting resuscitation. A red light swirled outside the doors, and in came the doctor, Dr. Peanut. He walked over. "What's up?" He checked his watch.

"One minute thirty seconds," said the nurse. She was small and wiry with chestnut hair.

"Okay, let's go ahead and disconnect. Let's get a tube in her pronto and prep some epi." Thelma's ECG had gone haywire, registering ventricular fibrillation. She made gurgling noises.

Another nurse had pushed the crash cart over with the cardioverter, which Dr. Peanut ramped up to 200 joules. They stood, waiting for the hypoxia to kill off her brain.

When five minutes hit, Thelma was lifeless. The ventilator had arrived, and Sawyer intubated her, squirting the epi down the tube. He then shocked her once, twice, and the nurse gave her breaths of 100 percent oxygen with the Ambu bag. The ECG squiggled, and Sawyer shocked her again. Boom, and there it was, a slow sinus rhythm. Perfect. The nurse hooked Thelma to the ventilator and checked her pupils, which were dilated and very sluggish. She would live, but not to tell the story.

~

Bard jumped from the loading dock, and Jack followed, hitting the grassed-over pavement hard.

He grunted and ran for his life. He looked over his shoulder, and Ismael was gaining on them, gripping the rucksack and a box of granola bars. There was no cover for 150 feet, but soon they entered scrub and then trees. Bard stopped, and Ismael caught up. Jack heaved, trying to catch his breath. It was the first sprint of his life, and he gasped. In the distance, the helicopter engine still whined. All were squatting, and Bard peered through the trees.

"Nothing yet, but let's skedaddle." Bard took off at a brisk pace, heading left and northwest.

For half an hour, they trotted downhill, the helicopter in the air, searching as they wound their way through hardwoods and crossed two small streams and a culvert with a gaping tunnel. Bard led the way into the concrete tunnel, filled with rocks and two inches of dank water. Camel crickets crawled above them.

"Let's hunker down for a while, until the helicopter leaves," said Bard.

"I think we shook them," said Ismael. "Here have one of these." He produced the faded box of granola bars wrapped in foil. "Should be good."

Jack watched them peel back the wrappers to reveal crumbly chunks. He did the same, poured it into his mouth, and chewed. It was peanut butter, a new taste, and he marveled. "God, that's good."

"Yeah, buddy," said Bard. "There's six in all, so let's save three. When it gets dark, we'll go back. We need food."

"What about water?" said Jack. He was parched.

"The stream's on the way back. We'll have to

wait," said Ismael. He fingered his goatee.

Jack's heart soon ceased to scud, and he sat on a dry rock, his ankles bursting with tenderness. He tied the laces on his new wet boots and admired his new friends.

"So, what exactly are we headed for?" said Jack. "It seems like we're getting farther away from Pan. I really need to help Lura escape, if that's even possible."

"Well," said Bard. His big yellow teeth looked gray in the dim light. "They'll be expecting to find you close to home, especially now. Could be they saw three sets of prints in the dust back at the wama. They might put two and two together and figure that we found you, but maybe not."

"Maybe hide out for a couple of weeks and head back," said Ismael. "We have the radio. Most likely it'll have to be an inside job."

Bard nodded and coughed, standing stooped over. "Wish we could eat these damn crickets."

"Well, I'll do whatever it takes," said Jack. "Lura's blood is on my hands, if it comes to that."

"Lord, the power of womenfolk," said Bard. "Well, I guess you did get her in a pickle. We need to get the Uprights in Pan on our side somehow, build a movement maybe, overthrow the whole lot."

Ismael laughed. "You and your revolutions."

"Don't laugh, boy. It can be done. There was that uprising back east in North Carolina, right? Wiped out a whole dome, although plenty of Uprights wound up dead. Right after that, they started giving us a day off once a week, and that seems to have shut the people up. Grasping at straws is what it is. I guess sometimes a little seems like a lot." He spat into the pooled water.

As darkness fell, the three emerged from the tunnel and made their way back to the wama, coming up behind an old dumpster. The back door had been closed and locked.

"Shit, they want us to go in the front door," said Bard.

"No choice," said Ismael.

Jack's nerves were up and his hands shaking. "What should we do?"

"Go around front, just one of us, then come and open the back door. Be careful of booby traps, though. Who volunteers?"

Ismael shouldered the rifle. "Me first. Give me five minutes."

"Right on, brother," said Bard.

Ismael finished his granola bar and ran down the length of the long building, stopping at the corner and peering around. There was still oatmeal in his throat, and he swallowed a few times. Keeping close to the building and watching his feet, he scurried forward, passed large garage doors, coming to the front. Now lit by the moon, he surveyed the vast empty parking lot that sprouted tall grass and weeds. Gathering his nerve, he waited and then dashed past a few old, rusted buggies, a closed double door, and stopped before entering the main doors, which had been blown out. Glass littered the ground. He tiptoed, rifle forward, looking for signs of an ambush. They could have left some Squad there, but the Infirm's lackeys were afraid of the dark, and he focused most on a trap. The inside of the wama loomed cavernous. He needed another rucksack and food.

Ismael walked through the doors and into the vacuous space. He knew the aisles by heart and made his way to pick up two small backpacks in the Back-to-School section. In the men's department, he nabbed a coat for Jack. The inside of the vast building seemed like a ship underwater, navigable only by touch. He made his way to the food aisles, trotting and then feeling for a bag of coffee. Two aisles over, he piled cans of what he wasn't sure into a backpack. He kept moving, grabbing a large jar of peanut butter, more granola bars, he thought, and cellophane packets of dried noodles, which they generally ate uncooked. With the two packs full, he made his way to the back door. Just as he was about to enter the stock room through swinging doors, he saw a tiny prick of light and froze. He heard voices, as if a joke were being told. He moved backward and bumped into a stack of canning jars, which rattled. His heart leaped, and he moved an aisle over and ducked behind a box filled with brooms, clutching his goods.

The door flew open, and three Squad burst through, stun guns at the ready. They paused and fanned out, running with headlamps blaring. Ismael had his eyes closed, but then opened them and made an instant decision. He walked toward the swinging doors, peered through, and seeing nothing, slipped inside. It was pitch black, and he fumbled his way to the back door, opening it with a screech. Below the unloading platform, he spotted the dumpster and jumped down with the backpacks.

"They're inside," he said. "We have to go, quick." He handed Jack a backpack.

Without speaking, the three ran the way they had come in, soon entering the shadows of trees. Bard led the way, pushing through brush and briars. On they moved, for nearly an hour, before Jack said they had to stop and rest beside a stream. He was wheezing, carrying the pack full of cans. In the woods, a few crickets chirruped as if stoned by the cold.

"Sorry, guys," said Jack. "Out of shape."

"Yeah, we're safe, I think," said Bard. "Take your time. Get some water."

Jack and Ismael drank. Then Bard.

"Shit, those Squads were taking it easy. Lucky for us. I think they were playing cards," said Ismael.

"Dumbasses," said Bard. "They're about as loyal as we were." He laughed.

"I bet we could convert 'em, if we had a chance," said Ismael.

"Well," said Bard, "we've got some on the inside that are about ready to change teams. We can only hope."

Jack spoke. "Might be good to have insiders, to rescue Lura."

"Lura could be a lost cause," said Bard. "I'm all for justice, but her days sound numbered."

Ismael nodded in the moonlight.

"Hell, I thought you guys were in," said Jack. "That's what's been keeping me going, Lura. And if we can save her, we can probably save others. Strange to say, though, I do miss my shower every day."

"Yeah, Jack, but we can't let some pussy determine our fate. We get caught, and that's the end. We'll end up in the Scrumptious recipe."

Jack smirked. "Get real. Lura is a person, not just some pussy. Yeah, I only generally saw her when she was naked in the shower, but there's more to it. I ambushed her in a sense. She's collateral damage because of me. It's the right thing to do."

"Right now, though, we have to focus on not getting caught," said Ismael. "Let the fire die down. You'll have to trust us. We have to work together."

"Just frustrated is all," said Jack. "Thanks for the coat, by the way."

"I get you," said Bard. "We missed our radio session today, but first thing in the morning, we'll check in, see what the situation is on the inside. The place could be on fire for all we know."

"With all of the oxygen used by the Infirm, it would just be one big fireball," said Jack.

"Yeah, that dome in Cleveland, Tennessee, went up in a hurry. Killed just about everybody," said Bard.

"I bet the sickos who survived had a field day with rank," said Ismael. "Nothing gets more points than a severe burn, especially on the head, except maybe schizophrenia. Never understood that."

They talked on for another hour, the cold hovering above freezing, and soon settled onto piles of pine straw. Jack wished for a strong dose of Champy and drowsed, unable to sleep.

~

Wednesday, dope day, emerged cloudy. The heat generators were working overtime to keep the dome at a pleasant 72. Giant recirculation tubes whooshed, producing a slight breeze in the streets.

Lura bolted at the 6:30 alarm in the hall, her head brushing the top of the cell. Below her, Mae was snorting, oblivious to the sharp tone. The day-shift guard walked the length of the hallway, yelling for everyone to get up, bright-eyed and bushy-tailed. He paused in front of Lura's cell.

"Hey! Lady Lura. You've got an appearance today. Be ready in five." He was plump and feisty in his gray uniform. His name was Gomer.

Lura wasn't sure what he meant. She slid down and checked the Scrumptious bin, two bars. She took one and chewed, getting herself a cup of water. The cubes had the same dull flavor as she was used to. Mostly, the cubes contained corn and alfalfa, but it was rumored that the Scrumptious contained human flesh and bones of the deceased. She had to use the toilet and bad, and waited until the guard was out of sight, but he was back as if waiting.

"Looking good, inmate!" Gomer stared at her through the bars, chuckling. "Gotta lift up to wipe, don't you? Well, don't worry. I've seen it all."

"Go to hell," said Lura.

Mae stirred in her bunk and gazed at the guard, then at Lura. "Get the fuck away," she said. "Goddamn pervert."

"Watch it. You'll be down in the hole before long." Gomer smirked and walked away, rubbing the back of his round head.

Lura finished her business. "Thanks."

"Yeah, whatever," said Mae. "These goddamn pillows are so thin they could make me scream," and she did.

"Pervert there said I had an appearance today," said Lura.

"That'll be fun. Just pray it's not the judge you castrated." Mae laughed. "I admire you, sister, but wouldn't want to be you."

"Anything special I should know?"

"Not, really. Just confess is the best you can do. They got it on camera, no doubt, plus the evidence in the judge's mouth. Oh, sister!"

Lura slumped onto the edge of the commode. "Yeah, but I wasn't there. That guy, Jack, he did it. He basically carried me out of my room. I was out of my mind on Champy."

"But why did he pick you? He had to have a reason. That judge is gonna make someone pay, and that Jack is long gone if he has any smarts. Better to starve to death if you ask me."

Images of Jack in the shower. His long neck had seemed to make him tentative but intelligent. His tight body. "Shit. Why me is a good question. He wanted to take me with him, but I couldn't make it into the sewer. He just left me there, the goddamned fool." Lura pinched her thigh. "Ow! Dammit!"

"Just settle down, girl, and let what comes come.

There's nothing you can do about it, unless Jack can come fetch you on his magic horse."

Lura finished her Scrumptious and slicked her teeth with her tongue to get rid of the grit. She paced in the cell, and then the guard was there, telling her to back up and put her hands behind her. She looked to Mae, and Mae nodded for her to do it. Soon, she was cuffed and walking down the hall, passing through a locked door, down another hall, jeers from the cells, and then into a small square room with a high ceiling and a Chatty on the wall. The guard left her there without any instructions.

At least there was a chair secured to the floor, and she sat, staring at the screen. It was a video of a bear eating a fish. For ten minutes, she sat there, and then the screen blipped. She stared at the array of three faces, all very serious and drawn, Cornelius Fava of Central, sitting in the middle of two dome judges. Lura recognized Fava. He was the only black person on the Central Committee, the chief, and she felt that she was in over her head.

"Good morning, Lura. You are Lura? Yes?" said Fava. His head was nearly resting on his right shoulder. He had sickle cell anemia in addition to his other charms.

"Yes, sir, that's me," said Lura.

"Well, as you may know, I am Cornelius Fava, the head of Central, and joining me today are two colleagues from the court. Judge Buttram and Judge Turnipseed." The judges stared into the camera, lips drawn, teeth showing. Buttram's liver quivered outside of his body, encased in a plastic shield. Turnipseed was blind, a paraplegic, and had bladder cancer. "As you may know, Judge Spurlock is currently indisposed, but he may very well be ready to take this case once his surgeries are complete."

Oh shit. Lura kept a straight face. "I see."

"So, Mrs. Lura, you have been summoned here today to receive your charges and enter a plea. Are you ready?"

Lura looked around the room. What could she say? "I'm ready, but let me say that I'm—"

"You'll have the opportunity for comment when directed to do so." Fava paused to let his Upright wipe the drool from the corners of his mouth. "The charges are as follows: Accessory to attempted homicide and fleeing Squad. We also have you down for resisting arrest, but the effects of Champy may be considered as a possible cause for leniency on that charge alone. Do you understand the charges?"

"Yes, sir, I get it," said Lura.

Fava said, "The esteemed Judge Turnipseed."

Turnipseed never wavered in his stare at the camera. His eyes rolled slightly back. "What is your plea?"

Lura thought. "Well, not guilty. I was abducted after the attack and physically carried to the park by the perpetrator, Jack. It was random. We had never met before except in the showers and the library."

"Did you not flee Squad?" said Buttram. His moist liver thumped with the beating of his heart.

"No, sir, I did not. I was carried. I was out of it, hallucinating from the Champy." Lura wrung her hands.

"Where," said Cornelius, "do you believe that the accused, Jack, is headed? What do you know? Has he been in contact?"

"I have no idea. I've never said two words to him. I told you that I was abducted, kidnapped. He should be charged with that as well."

"Why did you allow the accused into your flat?" said Turnipseed.

"I don't know. It was the Champy. I was hallucinating." Lura sagged in the chair and arched her back.

"You know that if you are lying," said Fava, "that charge will be added to your case. But for now, we will enter your plea as not guilty. The esteemed Judge Turnipseed."

Turnipseed thrust his jaw. "Trial shall be set for two weeks hence, Wednesday, December 15, 2345, barring interdiction by the esteemed Judge Spurlock. The time of said trial shall commence at eight a.m."

"Am I free until then?" said Lura.

Cornelius laughed, then looked stern. "No, no, Mrs. Lura. That will not be allowed. Your duties will be covered by other Uprights. You shall remain in custody until further notice. Everything clear?"

"Ugh," said Lura. "It's clear, but I'm innocent."

"We shall see," said Cornelius. "Good day." The Chatty went blank, returning to the bear scratching a tree.

Lura stood, her hands cuffed, and tried the doorknob, but it was locked. The camera near the ceiling blinked red. Within minutes, the door opened, and it was the guard, Gomer.

"Well, got your ducks in a row?" said Gomer. He patted his belly. He'd just had a cup of hot water with a chunk of Scrumptious dissolved in it.

Lura stared at him. "They think I'm guilty. This is such a sham."

"Well, the wheels they be turning regardless," said Gomer. "Back to your cell, inmate."

Back in her cell, Lura filled in Mae with the proceedings.

"No interim punishment? Hell, they kept me in a room with the lights on for two days and the most horrible music playing. About drove me bonkers."

"So, why did you try to kill yourself?" said Lura. She climbed to her bunk and sat there, hunched over."

"Because I'm a fucking Upright, that's why. I get raped on Sundays by freaks, that's why. I wipe shit and clean up vomit on alcohol day, that's why. Haven't you ever thought about it?"

"Well, sort of, but I've never tried it. Would you want to be Infirm instead?"

Mae hit the wall. "Hell no! That's the problem. There's no in between. Drives me ape shit."

Lura nodded. "Well, it used to be that way. Seems strange somehow."

"Yeah, all because of that lunatic Jerry Lewis and his telethons. You've been to the museum."

"Uh-huh," said Lura. "It's beyond understanding why anyone would want to be Infirm, to be bound to a wheelchair."

"Well, there's big money in disability. That's the

secret, I think. An Infirm creates jobs and generates a shit ton of revenue. Us regular healthy folks are just in the way. But they couldn't do it without us, right?"

"Well, no. They'd be screwed," said Lura. She watched Gomer pass by.

"Damn straight," said Mae. "You sure you don't want to have sex? What you got to lose?"

"No, thank you," said Lura. "You'll have to find someone else."

"Yeah, old Gomer would give it a go if I let him. He trades for Champy." Mae laughed and coughed.

"So, have you had a hearing? You have a trial scheduled?" said Lura.

"Oh, yeah. Hearing my ass. They showed me the video where I was hanging myself. I'm an open and shut case. No doubt they'll reprogram me with pills and electricity, turn me into a happy camper."

Lura had met another Upright who'd been re-programmed. She wasn't sure why the woman had been reprogrammed, but she had that glassy look. There was a channel on the Chatty, a reality show about reprogramming.

"Well, though, there is one way to escape," said Mae. "I'd give anything to have a mental disorder. Those dudes have it easy, coming and going as they please. Don't even have patients to take care of."

"Yeah, I've always wondered about them. They live on the southside in those yellow flats. The In-firm think they're gods of some sort."

"Well, I've got the depression going for me. Who knows? I might spiral out of control with some kind of disorder. There's no upgrading for mental stuff, though. Has to be natural."

Lura was back on her bunk, wondering if there was a way to fake it.

A long, slow beep, and it was shower time.

~

Gretchen finished her Scrumptious, drank a glass of water, and headed to 5400. Wednesday was drug day, and she would start with the conjoined twins. Drug day could be relaxing, depending on the drugs. She knocked and entered with her ID.

The twins were in bed, looking away from one another, their stumps showing from beneath a thin blanket. "Hey!" they said in unison. The one with the most skull was Frieda, the other was Lola.

"Morning," said Gretchen. "You guys ready to get up?" The Chatty was giving the latest details on the search for Jack. He was still on the run but assumed now to be in the company of the Merry Woodsmen. Two Squad units were out instead of one, plus the helicopter. There was footage from the helicopter of the rolling hills covered with trees. Lura pushed the custom wheelchair to the bed. Maneuvering the twins was like trying to put two lobsters in a basket. The Chatty paused for a long look at the Great One, a close-up of his fat face with a jagged harelip. *The Lord may be my shepherd, but I still want a new computer.*

"I'm hawngry," said Frieda. She grabbed Lura's neck with one arm as she scooted them into the chair.

"You're always hawngry," said Lola, stringy black

hair covering her face. Sitting in the chair, the two looked like a wishbone.

Lola turned the chair to the Chatty and checked the bin. She retrieved the two blocks of Scrumptious and set about to feed the twins. They chewed and swallowed synchronously. Gretchen just stood there, feeding them the cubes until they were gone, then shot a glass of water into each of their stomach tubes. "Need a sip?"

"Yeah," they said together, and Gretchen held a glass of water for them to drink from, first one and then the other.

"Gotta poo," said Lola.

"For God's sake," said Frieda. "Is that all you think about?"

Gretchen was hoping to be spared the chore, but there it was. "Alright, sisters, you know the drill."

Gretchen pushed the wheelchair beside the toilet. The trick was to keep Frieda in the chair while Lola teetered on the commode. "Upsy daisy," said Gretchen, gripping Lola under her armpits. She slid her on and then pulled her green pants down with some effort. Lola grunted, and Frieda fumed, but soon all was well, and there was a whoosh and a tiny bell that went *ding*. The drugs had arrived. The folks at Central decided who got what, and it was always a guessing game.

"Oh, baby, let's get it on," said Frieda. She pulled back her long black hair.

"What we got?" said Lola, clapping her hands.

Gretchen took the package and read it. There was a syringe of liquid inside. "Ayahuasca." Her heart sank. The twins would be vomiting their guts out, sitting in front of the commode, hallucinating other worlds, and encountering spirits of the dead.

The twins sighed, but they took what they could get; otherwise, Wednesday would just be a big drag.

"Ready?" said Gretchen. She wanted to get it over with.

"Oh, baby," said Frieda. "Maybe I'll have brain sex with one of them jungle men."

"Don't be reaching and touching," said Lola. "You know how you get."

Gretchen held up the syringe: 10 cc. "Open wide," *you motherfuckers*. She squirted half of the solution into Lola's mouth and half into Frieda's.

"Tastes like cum," said Frieda, laughing.

"How would you know, dear sister?" said Lola. "I'm the one who gives the best head."

"Shut your face!" said Frieda. "I hate you." She had the larger skull, but Lola had bigger breasts.

Soon, the twins were glassy-eyed, their heart rates increasing, their respirations getting shallow, looks of nausea from both. Gretchen had other patients in 5400 to dope. For those who took ayahuasca, she would have to return and check on them at intervals. She glanced at her watch. She'd been there nearly thirty minutes. First to heave was Lola, closely followed by Frieda. Deftly, they coordinated their vomiting, hitting the toilet nearly head-on. Gretchen held her breath, afraid she would vomit, and hurried from the room.

Her next patient was a woman in her fifties who was picky about the drugs she would take.

Her name was Betty Armistead, and she had short black hair tinged with gray. Her face was broad, and her lips sagged at the corners. Her distinguishing feature was a steel arrow that passed through her skull, exiting just above her ear. She also had three .22 caliber bullets lodged near her spine, which had partially paralyzed her. Her number had come up in the lottery for transformation, and she'd opted to move into the realm of the Infirm. Gretchen buzzed herself in.

"About time, girl," said Betty. The entrance and exit wounds of the arrow still leaked clear fluid, and she kept a headache because of it.

"First case of the day was ayahuasca. You know how that goes."

"Lord, none of that for me." She wheeled herself with one arm toward the bin. "Let's see what the doctor ordered. "Hear, you read it."

"Oh, good, rock cocaine," said Gretchen. "You ready to fire it up?" She glanced at the Chatty. Jack's face loomed large, first the front, then the side views. Then there was a photo of his accomplice, Lura, her ID picture. She looked sad, with an oval face and hair parted in the middle.

"Gonna make me cough," said Betty. "But let's get it going."

From a small drawer beneath the bin, Gretchen retrieved the glass pipe and a lighter. There were four large rocks, and she dropped one in. Betty could use her left arm, and she took the pipe and held it to her lips. Gretchen held the flame beneath the bowl at the end. Soon, the rock was smoking, and Betty inhaled, coughed, and inhaled again, holding in the smoke. Right away, her heart kicked into overdrive, and her face relaxed.

"Some good shit," said Betty. The pipe slipped from her hand and fell onto her lap. "Dammit." Her pupils weirdly dilated, giving her a vacant look.

"Keep her going," said Gretchen. She fired it up again and watched Betty gulp the vapor.

"Damn, I feel good, but getting antsy," said Betty. She puffed again, and the rock was nearly gone. "You coming back, right? In a couple hours?" The arrow in her head brushed her shoulder.

Gretchen nodded. "Just need to make the rounds, eight more to go. Mind if I take a hit?" She needed it, but was not allowed, being confined to Champy.

"Sure, girl. I know how hard you got it. Been there. Take a draw."

Gretchen hit the lighter and then took in the last of the vaporized rock. She held it as long as she could and blew out, sighing, coughing. "I appreciate it...really."

"Yeah, just don't forget to come back. I'd hate to report you."

Gretchen frowned. "Look, I know my job. No threats. You help me out, I help you out."

"Don't get your panties in a wad, girl. Go on. Do your job. I'll be here." Her speech was slightly slurred. "Damn, I feel good. But I'll feel like shit in an hour."

Gretchen nodded and turned to the Chatty. It was breaking news. The helicopter had spotted the fugitives, one suspected to be Jack. She wished her life were that exciting and exited into the quiet hall, headed for the next Infirm.

~

At daybreak, Bard was up, the radio sitting on a flat piece of limestone. He had thrown a stone over a branch tied to the antenna wire. Jack, on his side, aching to get up, but cold and shivering, stayed put in his misery. Ismael had built a small fire, surrounded by three rocks. He squatted there, holding his hands in fingerless gloves over the flames.

"Get on up, sleepy head," said Bard. "Gonna make contact on the inside."

Jack pushed straw off his legs and tried to stand. His whole body ached, and he fell back onto his elbow. "Hell."

"About got you whooped, don't we?" said Bard. He laughed. He cranked the charger on the small black radio, which made whirring sounds. He cranked for a full five minutes, resting every minute or so. He checked his watch, only four minutes till check-in. He flipped a switch, and a blue light glowed behind a circular dial. There was a detachable microphone with a stretchy cord.

"What's for breakfast?" said Jack. He hugged himself against the cold and stood in a narrow beam of sunlight.

"Oatmeal," said Ismael, "and maybe one of these cans of tomatoes." He held up the can, the label yellow and peeling.

"What're tomatoes?" said Jack.

"I don't know," said Ismael, "but they're tasty.

Kind of mushy and tart."

"Beggars can't be choosers," said Bard. He turned up the volume, listening to the distant whoosh. He tilted the radio and hit the button to search for any active transmission. The numbers reeled by and stopped. Bard put his finger to his lips. It was a transmission between Pan and Laramore, a daily census update. He held the radio to his ear, conserving the battery. After a minute, he put the radio down. "They've got an imbalance issue. Need more Upright in Pan. Gonna transfer six from Laramore, fifty grand apiece."

"Just like buying a damn salad," said Ismael.

"Shh," said Bard. "Tuning in." He held the scan button until it hit the 600s and then tapped until he reached 612.550. He turned up the volume and sat back, leaning against a white pine with the radio between his legs. He clicked the microphone five times and waited.

Then there it was. "Fire and ladder, pronto. Fire and ladder, pronto."

Bard grinned. "Pronto, lemon squeezebox. Pronto, lemon squeezebox."

"Got you," said the voice. "You've got sixty seconds. Central is on high alert. Squad moving."

"Confirm, Jack, present and accounted for. Headed toward Laramore. Advise?"

"Keep covered, squeezebox. New developments inside."

"Ask about Lura," said Jack.

"Status on Lura," said Bard.

"The accomplice in custody, awaiting trial.

Grim."

"Requesting rescue mission," said Bard. "She's innocent."

"Impossible on this end, without help."

"Plan forward," said Bard. "Will stay near Laramore for two weeks."

"Mission to be discussed. One last reply."

"Play hard," said Bard, and the connection was lost. He shut off the radio. "You know, this Lura character just might be what we need."

"What's that mean?" said Jack.

"I mean, we're the Merry Woodsmen. The rumor is that we'll be back and bring down the house. That we'll overthrow the dome. This just might be the cause we need. Thus far, we've been happy with little schemes, shutting down power and so forth."

"Look, I don't need revolution. I just want to do what's right by Lura," said Jack. "The Infirm have weapons and punishments."

Ismael spoke. "But she's done for, as you've said. It could be harder to extract her alone than it would be to bring the whole dome down."

Bard grinned. "Yeah, what he said." He slid the radio into a sleeve and then into the rucksack. "This could damn well be glorious. I thought they'd laugh when I brought it up. Damn boy, welcome to the Merry Woodsmen."

"We need to move, though, for now, farther from Pan," said Ismael. He had opened the tomatoes and placed the can over the coals. The oatmeal was cooling.

"You know," said Bard, "them transferring Uprights from Laramore could be an opening in the armor. Most likely fly over in copters and then pass through the cargo gate. We can arrange a diversion of some sort. Still need inside help, though." He ate a few spoons of oatmeal and handed the wooden spoon to Jack. "Dig in, boy. Long day of hiking coming up."

Jack ate his share and passed the pot to Ismael. "Getting good vibes about this rescue. So, what? We set it up like she's been falsely accused? Maybe turn her into a martyr to get the Uprights in line?"

"Something like that," said Bard. He watched Ismael stir the tomatoes with a stick. "You've got to come clean, though, let it be known that you kidnapped her, that it was a big mistake on your part, that she's innocent. Right?"

"Yeah, I can do that, for her, sure. It's the whole truth." He took the hot pot from Ismael and nearly dropped it. He smelled it and then hoisted a juicy plum tomato into his mouth. He made a face. "Never had nothing like it." He ate one more and passed the can.

"When's the transfer of Uprights?" said Ismael.

"Looks like two weeks. Lots of paperwork that goes with it, health screenings, and so on. Not nearly enough time to set an entire revolt in progress, but maybe enough time to extricate Lura." Bard slurped down a tomato. "That could just serve as step one, a bold move by the Merry Woodsmen, get the Uprights talking between their teeth."

"If we get her," said Ismael, "it'll be all over the Chatty. The Infirm love their breaking news."

The helicopter was beating the air in the distance.

"Shit, fellas, we gotta move, find some cover." Bard hefted the rucksack.

Ismael chugged the juice in the can and covered it with pine straw. "Let's move."

Jack wasn't quite ready, but he threw on the backpack and followed. The helicopter grew louder, and the trees were thinning. Bard stopped dead at a small meadow with knee-high grass. He backtracked and skirted the open area, hunting for thicker tree cover, but the helicopter was coming straight for them.

"Down! Get down! Get small!" said Bard. He looked up into the clear, bright sky punctured by tall pines. The helicopter was circling and then hovering as if they'd been spotted. "Shit."

The copter spun back and descended in a slow circle, headed for the open meadow.

"Now we run," said Ismael, and he took the lead, leaping over mushroomed logs and barreling through thick green briars that tore at his plaid wool coat. Bard was right behind, and then Jack, half running, half limping with his sore ankles. On they pushed, Jack wheezing, gulping for air. The helicopter noise faded, and they crossed an old road, hit a culvert, and scrambled around an old bridge buttress.

"Look for train tracks!" said Bard.

They tumbled forward, Jack slipping behind. He conjured an image of Lura in the shower, her perfect breasts, her mound of pubic hair, her short brown hair parted in the middle. He surged and nearly ran over Bard.

"This way," he said, and they were off again, running when possible, sometimes just trotting, getting slower as they climbed up short steep hills. Up ahead was a ridgeline that towered a few hundred feet overhead. "Here," said Bard. The tracks and crossties had been removed, but the raised gravel bed was still there, overgrown with grass and saw palmetto.

The sound of the helicopter was back.

"Damn," said Jack. He stopped, put his hands on his knees, and panted.

~

With news of Jack's sighting, Central was hopping. Two units of Squad had been flown out, and the chase was on. Cornelius Fava sat reclined in his wheelchair in his room, gabbing back and forth with the Central members, keeping a live feed from the search party on a private channel, mainly audio, but with some video. The voice was that of Colonel Faccia. Fava wondered about the loyalty of Squad. Bard and Ismael had been Squad at one point and had deserted. Others could do the same.

"Okay, we're back up," said the Colonel. "One Squad in pursuit. Will drop the second ahead of the group. Circle them. They're as good as caught." He was the highest-ranking Upright in Squad, his judgment deemed flawless and trustworthy by the Council, especially Cornelius Fava.

"Damn, this is exciting," said Leroy Smalls from his chair. He strained to picture the scene, his gummy eye slits oozing. His personal Upright was beside him, detailing the video footage.

The Colonel spoke. "Landing now. An old overpass. Squad to be released."

"Any further sightings?" said Fava, his head glued to his shoulder.

"No, sir, but they're in the vicinity," said the Colonel. "Squad disembarking." A short video feed of bridge pilings amid trees.

On the streets of Pan, Squad moved to cover the main lanes, sixty in all, all men except for two women. The Uprights could use the uproar to stage an uprising. It was essential to keep order.

Remy, a lanky Squad, walked with his stun gun charged. Beside him was Kate, short and stocky with muscled forearms. They spoke as they walked, looking straight ahead. Remy coordinated the covert radio contact with the Merry Woodsmen. In all, there were seven in the group, sworn to secrecy, minnows swimming with the fish. The ongoing search played in small earbuds.

"Think they'll make it?" said Kate. She gazed around, looked up at the buildings, and spotted cameras at every intersection. The auto ID scanners.

"No clue, but Bard and Ismael are pretty slick. They know the area like an Infirm knows his butt. That Jack is in good company, but he could be slowing them down." Remy noticed two Uprights standing near one another in front of a café, The Happy Pilgrim. He walked toward them and motioned for them to separate, which they did, hurrying away.

"The judge should be getting his new jewels and

scepter any time now," said Kate.

"Yeah, and he'll get rank because of it. Rots my gut," said Remy. "Okay, have to separate here. Tomorrow, alcohol day, the Council should be sloshed. I think they skipped out on the drugs due to the developments. We'll gather at the usual place. Get info about this Lura. Learn what you can."

Kate nodded and left Remy at the intersection of Fifth and Seventh, headed up one block. The scanners beeped as she passed. Up ahead was an Upright. She recognized him as 52. No one seemed to know his first name. She stepped off the sloped curb and approached.

"Hey, fifty-two. No work today? Can't have you idling in the streets." She raised her eyebrows.

"Oh, sorry, ma'am. My apologies. All of my patients were pill poppers this morning. Just pop and drop. I'm on my way to head back and follow up."

"Excellent," said Kate. She moved in closer, her hands on her hips as if about to let loose. "Lura. What do you have?"

Fifty-two held up his hands as if surrendering, then whispered. "Clean as a pin. Kidnapped for sure. Wrong place, wrong time. Oh, and this. Her parents are elites, but she doesn't know it yet." He made a cuckoo sign with his hand.

"Interesting. Could be worth something." She changed her demeanor. "Okay, fifty-two! Move along like you're told. Back to work, bucko."

Fifty-two stifled a grin. "Yes, sir! I mean, yes, ma'am!" He backed away as if about to be stunned.

"Cocksucker," she said, in case anyone was

listening.

~

Jack lagged behind, lumbering as if lead weights ringed his neck. He hit his shoulder against a tall tulip tree and gasped. The tree didn't budge. He realized he was hot, even though it was still in the forties, and he struggled to run and pull down the coat zipper at the same time. The helicopter had passed over and faded. He looked up, and ahead were more bridge buttresses. Bard was a good fifty feet in front of him.

"Halt!"

And it was like train cars stopping and colliding.

Bard said, "Fuck," eyeing the Squad with his stun gun drawn.

Ismael was quick, though, and had a bead on the Squad's forehead. Two others appeared from the dense underbrush.

"Halt!" repeated the Squad.

Bard eyed the rifle barrel edging just beyond his shoulder. With his hands up, he stepped sideways. "We're halted. What's the goddamn problem? We're out for a hike, and you come along." He spat.

The Squad glanced at one another.

"Put the gun down," said one. They all wore light gray suits made of a flexible material, dark stripes on the legs. Their belts held a variety of po-licing tools, including cuffs and a baton.

"You'll let us pass first," said Ismael. "You can stun us, but I can kill you. Bullet with your name on it, right here." He relaxed his eyes and let the barrel swing to the Squad's chest.

"Like hell," said the largest one. He was Dirk, muscled with a red face and chapped lips. He licked them and grimaced. He then spoke into the mic on his chest.

"Shit, he's calling the copter," said Bard. "Look, we're all Uprights here. Let's stick together. No one has to get hurt. No one has to know that you decided to spare your own life and let us pass."

Dirk frowned a frowny frown. "Bullshit, you traitor. You used to be Squad. Deserter."

Bard laughed. "Do you really mean to tell me that you enjoy taking orders from freaks with assholes on their faces? Why would you turn against your own kind? We're brothers, you and me."

"I'll tell you—"

A shot cracked from the rifle, and the bullet sheared off a chunk of bark behind Dirk's head. All three Squad flinched and stepped back.

"You fucker," said Dirk. He looked to his comrades for support, but they stood listless. Dark circles of sweat outlined his armpits. "You know the penalty would be death for all of you. I tell you what. Give us Jack there, and we'll let you slip away. What do you say?"

"Don't think so," said Bard. "We're the Merry Woodsmen. All for one and one for all. We've got your number, and you know it. We're already pinned for death. Nothing to lose by wasting you fuck ups. Do the right thing and let us pass. We'll be even, like you never saw us, although you've already been transmitting. So, move aside, or my buddy Slim here will start low and work his way up to your thick skulls."

Jack marveled at Bard's speech. He wanted to give him a high five for effort, but didn't really expect to be allowed to pass. He wiped sweat from his eyes, feeling refreshed and ready to sprint if needed.

Bard frowned. "I'll count to three, real slow. On three, my buddy here will let loose. He's a prime shot. He can knock down a pinecone from fifty feet. Your choice."

The Squads looked at each other. Dirk seemed ready to do his own countdown. "I dare you, brother."

Bard went serious. "One...two..."

No one moved.

"Three."

A shot rang out, and one of Dirk's sidekicks went down, howling, clutching his knee.

"The fuck?" Dirk went from a vague smile to terrified and stumbled over to his downed compatriot. "Alright, then, go, go, just git and be gone. Enough of your games. But you'll never live this down. I promise."

Bard laughed. Ismael laughed. Jack just looked blank as Bard led the way, making a semicircle around the terrified Squad. And then he broke into a run with Ismael and Jack in tow.

After two hours of running downhill and trudging uphill, Jack yelled out that he was done. He needed to rest. The helicopter they'd heard in the distance was now quiet.

Bard and Ismael seemed glad that Jack had

halted them and dropped to the ground, breathing hard. Without speaking, Bard pulled off the rucksack and hauled out two liter bottles of stream water. Ismael found the granola bars, and they feasted in the afternoon sunlight, fingering down through the pines, big leaf magnolia, and holly. All was quiet, save the heavy breathing.

Bard pulled a topo map from the rucksack and a small compass. He arranged the map to point north and pointed to their destination, the dome at Laramore. "Thataway," and he pointed to the west.

They rested for fifteen minutes and were about to head out when came a tremendous crashing sound.

"Deer!" said Ismael. He pointed, and three large does were streaking through the forest.

"Holy cow," said Jack. "Scared the bejesus out of me. Never seen one before. Can you eat them?"

"Yeah, but all we got is this little twenty-two. Wouldn't do much," said Bard. He moved forward, stepping around a patch of dark green lichen that looked like a mini forest. "We make another two hours, and we'll call it quits," he said over his shoulder. Should be a small lake in half an hour."

They plodded on, the day warming, but the sun soon began its dip, and the chill that would follow was evident. They traversed a hill overlooking the green lake and covered another good five miles before reaching a gap. The wind blew there, and Bard led them farther down near a small creek scattered with beech trees, one that had fallen, but still growing along the damp, cold ground.

Jack was the first to unload his pack and sit. He pulled off his boots and examined the burst blisters on his heels and the ends of his toes. He groaned, thinking about having to wear his boots to keep his feet warm.

They risked a fire, and Ismael tended to that, while Bard and Jack gathered wood. Soon, the fire was crackling, just in time to greet the chill of the long night. Jack tried to squat on his haunches but pulled a large rock close to the fire. Dinner would be something called Hamburger Helper, still viable after years on the shelf.

"So, how many on the inside are you working with?" said Jack.

"Seven Squad that I know of," said Bard, "and about twenty Uprights. One is the personal Upright of a Council, the little guy without eyes. She's a boatload of information, hates the Infirm with a passion."

"Damn," said Jack. "So what can happen? I mean, how would we go about rescuing Lura and creating this revolt?" He held one foot to the fire, then the other, when he could smell the leather burning.

Ismael sighed. "Bard?"

"I think it has to be after she's officially sentenced, which will most likely be death. Makes me queasy thinking about it. We let the wheels of justice turn as long as we can, though. The people will be hot. Hasn't been an execution since this one guy, you know about it, smothered his Infirm with a pillow and choked him with a shoelace. About ten years ago, right?"

Jack remembered. They'd hanged the poor guy in the middle of the street, hoping to teach the Uprights a valuable lesson. There had been spotty unrest, and Squad had been sent to the streets for a week afterward to keep the peace.

Bard watched Ismael stirring the Hamburger Helper with water in their single pot. "Better make two boxes. We got a long hike tomorrow."

Ismael nodded.

"So," said Bard. "We let the hammer fall and get the people riled up and into the streets. That'll occupy Squad. From there, who knows? The folks on the inside will have to work that out."

Jack stood to avoid the smoke in his face. "So, what's our role here, boss? I mean, what do we do? How can we help?"

Bard chuckled. "Well, she has to go somewhere, right? We'll be that somewhere, and then we'll be the Merry Woodspeople. We'll have to be ready."

"And then what? The dome collapses. The Infirm die, and the Uprights take over?" said Jack.

"Who knows?" said Ismael. "Of course, they'd send in the feds and murder every last one of them."

"That seems worse than just Lura catching hell," said Jack. "I don't want people to die. I'm trying to prevent that." He rubbed his long neck and sat on his rock. "Damn, that smells good. I think the best part about being with you guys is eating this strange food." He took a drink from the water bottle and looked up through the branches at the fabric of stars.

"Well, something has to give," said Bard. "The Infirm are bat-shit crazy. I mean, Uprights are basically slaves, even though they go home at the end of the day. One dome falls, then maybe another. Maybe all they get is another day off. The rot has got to stop, though." He threw a chunk of wood into the fire, sending up sparks.

"Just a couple minutes," said Ismael, stirring the bubbling pot.

"Got my mouth watering," said Jack. "So, what if a bunch of Uprights escape into the woods? Maybe we could start a colony, be independent that way."

"They'd never let that happen. They'd bring in the big guns and wipe us out." Bard laughed. "Gotta go sometime, though, fighting for what's right."

"I suppose," said Jack. He watched Ismael place the pot on the ground to cool. "So, what do you know about the rest of the world? The books in the library are only about nature and such. Are other countries this way? Are we still even a country?"

"I only know some things from when I was on Squad. We'd get invited to sessions. Sometimes they would be about other people in other countries trying to imitate us. We're the banner child, though. The world is a big place, bigger than you can imagine. There are oceans, where the water stretches for thousands of miles. Kind of freaky, but I'd like to see it one day. All we know is that damn dome and the infernal Infirm." He drank water from the metal bottle.

"Pisses me off. Why be Infirm when you can be healthy? I've never understood that," said Jack.

Ismael spoke. "For prestige, for the glory of the state. Money. For Jerry *fucking* Lewis."

"But, as far as I know, he was never Infirm," said Jack.

"Yeah, but he made it cool. People want to be a part of something, want to belong. Before he was through, every man, woman, and child was hankering to be in the spotlight, to be special." Bard spat. "Goddamn idiots."

"I get you," said Jack. "I fucking hate foot-care day."

"Oh, Jesus. That's why I went Squad, that and sex day. I couldn't take it, blowing some old man or shoving a dildo up some granny's ass."

"So, you did your time?" said Jack. The smoke was blowing in his face again, and he coughed.

"I'd say so," said Bard. "About ready, good buddy?"

Ismael grunted and picked up the pot with a loose glove. He took a spoonful and passed it to Bard. Bard ate a heaping spoonful and passed the pot to Jack, and around it went around four times, until it was finished.

"Damn, that's good stuff," said Jack.

"Can't beat the wama," said Bard. "Gonna soak my feet in the crick." He pulled off his worn boots and thick, dirty socks.

"That sounds like a plan," said Jack, and he joined him while Ismael washed the pot and put things away.

An owl hooted, and Jack cringed. "What the hell was that?"

Bard laughed. "Just an owl, my friend. A big bird with big eyes and a sharp beak. Comes out at night."

Jack was already cold, and dangling his feet in the icy water sent a chill through his body. "Oh, that's the ticket." He shivered. "Can't take it for long though. No critters in the creek I should worry about, is there?"

"Naw," said Bard. "Maybe some little fish, and I reckon they're sleeping, which we should do. We'll each take a watch. You want to go first? Three hours on."

"I'll need to show him how to use the gun," said Ismael.

"Yep, just in case. The Squad could be right on our balls, although I doubt it. But you never know." Bard let his feet drip before pulling on his socks, and Jack did the same.

~

Alcohol day, and 52 griped at the Chatty for waking him up. It was the glorious Great One, his privates freshly powdered. His eyes roamed in his huge, somewhat translucent head. The close-ups showed intricate nets of blue veins. *Vanilla pudding goes with just about anything.* Fifty-two gave the Chatty the finger and dropped his feet to the cool floor.

Fifty-two was fifty-three and had a gray comb-over. His face wrinkled when he smiled, and he wore glasses, which was unusual for an Upright. He felt that the glasses gave him a tiny advantage in his dealings with the Infirm. He'd not had Champy the night before and had slept poorly. He stuck his hand into the bin and pulled out a bar of Scrumptious and a small plastic bag. For thirty-four years, he'd been serving the Infirm, the same damn things every damn day. He figured they owed him Champy at the least. He chewed and swallowed, nearly gagging on his breakfast. Same old same old, but at least he'd received that night's Champy.

Dressed in his wrinkle-free blue uniform, he checked out of his room, descended a flight of stairs, and burst onto the street. Beyond the dome, he could tell that the sun was rising as it did every day without fail. He passed a few Uprights and soon arrived at 3400, his building for alcohol day, shitface day. He enjoyed pushing his patients to drink as much as they could and then watching them suffer the consequences. He wanted to scream.

Inside, 52 decided to start at the end of the quiet hall. The building was narrow, with flats on one side and the hallway on the other. Without knocking, he scanned himself into the flat of Beebee Barnswallow, pushing on the door, and it was unlocked.

Beebee was in bed, switching channels on the Chatty with the buttons behind her teeth. She was one unique specimen, a testimony to the daring of modern surgery. Basically, she had been sawn in half, everything vital shoved to the left. Her right arm and leg had been removed, as had half of her face and jaw, leaving the brain bucket, as she called it, intact. She kind of looked like a crooked stick. She suffered from the usual diabetes and high blood pressure. Her glaucoma was coming along nicely, and she would be blind within a few short years.

"Urgl, brgl," said Beebee. She only had half of

her tongue.

"Well, urgl burgl to you to, honey," said 52. The room smelled of feet, or rather, foot, and needed a deep cleaning, but he would never volunteer for that, waiting until ordered. He sat in her wheelchair and spun in a circle. The Chatty was giving the latest details on the hunt for the Merry Woodsmen and Jack. By now, everyone knew that one of the Squad had been shot in the knee and that they had slipped away. There had been much murmuring in the showers the day before. It had also been announced that Lura would be formally charged and then sentenced. This, along with the saga of the missing Uprights, was creating an undercurrent, a tingle, among the Uprights. This was just what was needed to divert them from their miserable lives. Who knew what might happen? At that moment on the Chatty, a panel of Infirm experts was batting the ball of confusion back and forth, speculating on the next move of the infamous trio.

"I think they plan to lead us on a wild goose chase," said an elfish man, a paraplegic with fulminating psoriasis, his skin covered in soothing white ointment. "And while we're busy there, something else will happen here. It's a decoy, a trap, I say." He scratched the side of his face and drew blood.

"The old switcheroo," said an enormous woman with no arms or legs and her large intestine sewn to the outside of her abdomen inside a clear plastic sheath. "But I say they should be caught soon. This is ridiculous, the Uprights being so slippery. Is it a lack of technology on our part?" She coughed, and her massive bosom quivered beneath a black stretch dress.

"You'd think," said a third. He was kind of average looking but had HIV, leukemia, a large sarcoma on his back, and only one lung and one kidney. His heart had been weakened as well, one of the coronary arteries blocked with a small balloon. "We should have brought out the big guns by now. I mean, they used a gun, and we should do the same. What are those shoulder things called, bazookas? I say bring out the bazookas, take 'em dead or alive." And that sent the conversation into overdrive.

"Bunch of crap," said 52. "You eat yet, babydoll?"

"Urgl, burgl," said Beebee. She shook her head no.

Fifty-two went to the bin and pulled out the Scrumptious, along with three 60-cc syringes filled with liquor, all at least 100 proof. He broke off a cube and held it to Beebee's mouth. She sucked it in with her narrow tongue and chewed. He fixed her a glass of water, which she drank with a red straw. It took her about ten minutes, but she finished her Scrumptious and then had 52 get her on the commode, where she peed like a racehorse and made a few brown friends. Fifty-two grimaced while cleaning her up and plopped her into the wheelchair.

"Urgl, burgl, urgl," said Beebee. Having only half a jaw made her look famished.

"Yeah, yeah, you want to get piss drunk, I know. And so do I. But where's my moonshine, I ask you? Didn't even get Champy last night. If this shit weren't laced with laxative, I'd be obliged to share with you, right? Just kidding."

Fifty-two knew what Beebee liked. He took one syringe and pushed it slow into the feeding tube protruding from her stomach. She liked to suck on the other syringe like a lollipop and save the third syringe for later in the day. Within thirty seconds, Beebee's eyes began to slowly crack like ice, and she shivered, the alcohol pulsing throughout. Fifty-two leaned her chair back, turned her on her side, and propped the second syringe near her head. He took a piece of silk tape and taped it there, the nipple within reach of her half mouth.

"Oh, babydoll, getting cranked for the day. Alright, babydoll, I'm outta here, moving on."

"Urrrglll, burrrglll," said Beebee.

He closed the door and skipped a door, an old man he didn't like, and scanned at the next door, knocking. The lock clicked open. "Well, for Pete's sake!" said 52. Poor Mr. Turnbuckle, Jesse to be exact, was on the floor, flat on his back. His false teeth with the call button lay beyond his reach. He was gifted with multiple sclerosis and lupus, which nearly killed him every few weeks, his organs fighting for life. To sweeten the pot, a large hole had been constructed through his chest that you could put your hand through. He'd sacrificed a lung for that. Plus, he had lots of interesting tattoos of mythical creatures. He was a ripe 116 and looked it, but still was sharp as a tack.

"Goddamn it," said Jesse. "Get me the hell up, boy."

There was a puddle of urine on the floor. "Huh,

who you calling boy, old man?" Fifty-two put his hands on his hips and laughed. "Lucky I came along. I was gonna save you for last."

"Lucky, my ass," said Jesse. "Get me up before I report you."

Fifty-two leaned down and grabbed the old man beneath his arms. He was light as a feather, and 52 swung him into the wheelchair. "You trying to walk and fall?"

"Trying to get some damn food. Been laying here since I heard the thump in the bin. Damn, my hip hurts. Might of broke it."

"Well, lucky you," said 52. "Let me check." He slid down the old man's slick blue pants. "Got a big old purple bruise there. Hurt?"

"Hurts like hell, what do you think?"

"Okay, now. I'll get X-ray over. You may need to go to the hospital and get your rank boosted. Maybe they'll just slice you off at the hip there."

Fifty-two retrieved the Scrumptious and the syringes of alcohol. He noted that one was bright red, pure grain alcohol, nearly 200 proof. "Damn, they're trying to kill you." He held up the red syringe. He then put the bar of Scrumptious in the old man's lap, and he ate it chunk by chunk, only finishing half, and then drinking half a glass of water.

"You need to drink more water, old man. Especially if you're gonna be drinking." Before injecting a tube of spirits into his feeding tube, he pumped in a big glass of water.

"Slow down, boy. That's making a pressure in my belly." He scrunched in the wheelchair like an old scarecrow.

"Yes, sir," said 52. He took the remote and dialed up the hospital channel on the Chatty. The face of a nurse appeared. Fifty-two filed an emergency visit request for the old man and his hip, and the nurse's face disappeared, replaced by a scene from an operating theater, a woman's small intestine being shortened to instill chronic diarrhea. "Yuck," said 52, shaking his head. "They'll be here pronto, sir, the X-ray and all. You ready to grease lightning?"

At that, Jesse laughed, losing his teeth onto his lap. "Dammit."

Fifty-two injected half of a clear syringe and then gave Jesse a taste. Jesse made a sour face, but grinned and took another. Soon his head was nodding, and 52 reclined him in the chair, headed to the next patient.

~

Lura hadn't slept well, used to getting her Champy even though the schedule was irregular. She was dying inside, craving a drug cocktail. Mae was snoring beneath her, had been snoring for what seemed like forever. There was nothing to do but watch the big Chatty through the bars in the hall. The channels changed randomly. She'd been staring at the Great One, asleep on his huge feather bed for nearly an hour. He'd opened his eyes and had begun to cry. She watched as a pair of hands injected a soothing solution into the Great One's IV that was taped to his head. *Loud cursing neither distracts nor agitates the venomous cobra.* She tried to imagine Jack, wondering what he was doing, if he was on the run or holed up with the other two. Why had he chosen her? Had it really been just a matter of chance? She remembered his honest face, his long neck, and his brown eyes. She'd seen him naked in the shower plenty of times, but that didn't really matter, although he had nice legs, and he didn't have that little paunch like most of the Upright men.

The channel switched to a documentary about Jerry Lewis. It was an MDA telethon from 1976. He was wearing a black suit and a white shirt with a black bowtie. His face looked tan, oily, wet. There was a live audience, standing, applauding him. Behind him, an easy-listening band played: flutes, clarinets, percussion, and trombones. Jerry snapped his fingers and broke into song, much to the delight of the audience. "See what joy you can bring, let's get those telephones to ring." Phone numbers ran on the bottom of the screen. "Oh, won't you call me. That's why I'm here." The audience clapped, smiling wildly. Over $18 million in donations and counting. Jerry broke into song again. By the late 2100s, there had been a telethon for just about every chronic disease and disorder.

Lura wanted to look away, but there were only the walls and ceiling. Gomer was on duty and passed by every ten minutes or so, tapping his fingers together, stopping to stare at her. He'd offered her Champy in exchange for a blowjob, but she'd refused, and now she thought better of it. She heard yelling from cells down the hall. Someone was singing along with Jerry and his guest, Dean Martin.

Mae snorted, awake and yawning and stretching

like a lion. "You there, sweetie?" Her feet hit the cold floor.

"Thank God," said Lura. "I'm about to go insane. I'd give anything to be out of here."

"What? You don't like my company?" Mae laughed.

"Well, not when you're snoring."

"Sorry, doll. I guess I'm used to this place. You checked the bin?"

"No, not even hungry. I feel like my brain needs something, though. God, this absolutely sucks."

"Well, you have that Jack character to thank for that. They'll catch him, though. Can't believe they shot a Squad. Serves 'em right, though."

"What if I said I had feelings for him, this Jack?" said Lura.

"You think he's gonna rescue you, whisk you away to Neverland? Maybe even have a baby." Mae laughed.

"Stop, but it wouldn't surprise me. I mean, he owes me. He looked so helpless when he dropped into that sewer."

"Left you high and dry, right?" Mae pulled down her baggy pants and sat on the toilet. The noise was terrific. "Sorry about that." She stood and flushed and went to the bars, staring at the wall. "Hey, Gomer!"

Gomer waddled over all roly-poly, his hand stroking the stun gun on his belt. His face was bright red as if he'd been drinking. Like the Infirm, he was allowed alcohol every day if desired, but only at the end of the day. "What's shaking?"

"Well, my titties, if you cooperate." She licked her big red lips and thrust out her chest.

Gomer purred. "What you need?"

"I think me and my friend here could use a little Champy. Got any?"

"Huh, needy, I see. Well, it'll cost you a feel and toots there can bend over and flash me her camel toe. I got you covered. Deal?"

Mae looked back at Lura, who was shaking her head no. "Look, doll, we do what we have to do. You need a lift, and so do I, or at least a push down." She turned back to Gomer. "You know what it is, sedative or the nightmare variety?"

"You got me. It all looks the same. Take your chances. You got five minutes to sort it out with your prima donna there." He walked away.

Mae batted her long lashes at Lura. "Look, we both need it. Do it for me. He just wants a peek, that's all."

"What if he decides to come in here and rape me?"

"Who, him? He doesn't have the balls. He's never laid a finger on me, except where I let him feel. Otherwise, we sit here all day, stone-cold sober."

Lura imagined her tiny flat, the small but comfortable bed, the noisy showers. She'd just been plucked from her room and thrown into this mess. "Okay, but just this once. Damn pervert. Feel like I'm in a dream."

"Gomer!" said Mae.

He was back in a hurry. Mae already had her top up, her round boobs with big tan nipples exposed.

Gomer seemed startled and stared. He put his hand through the bars and ran it all around, squeezing. He moved to the other and did the same. Mae stepped back but left her top up, giving him a bonus gaze.

"Alright," said Gomer. "The sassy one. Show me what you got." He grinned.

Lura frowned. She turned, pulled her pants down, and bent over.

"Spread those cheeks," said Gomer, a big hard-on visible in his pants.

Lura wanted to spit. She did as told and heard Gomer whistle.

"Baby, need some of that," said Gomer. His feet did a little tap dance. "Hey!" Lura had ended the show.

Mae was laughing. "Okay, buster, now hand it over. The Champy."

Grumbling, Gomer fumbled in his large back pocket and pulled out a bag with ten lozenges. He took four and handed them through the bars to Mae.

"Much appreciated, my little prince," said Mae. "See, doll, that wasn't so bad."

"God, give it to me," said Lura. Mae dropped two lozenges into her hand.

Mae put her two tablets beneath her pillow for later.

Lura ran a glass of water from the tap and dropped in the tablet. It fizzed, and she smelled the familiar lemon. "Here we go." She drank, crawled up into the bunk, and waited. It only took seconds for the drug to kick in. She felt woozy and leaned against the wall. She sighed, and an image of a playground, little boys with balls that had eyes and ears. She watched them frolic and lapsed into a deep sleep laced with sloths and rainbows.

~

After his uneventful watch, except for a tiny scorpion crawling on his leg, Jack had piled on the ground, wrapped in his coat, using a rotten log and pine straw as a pillow. He slept the sleep of the dead, dreaming deeply that he was back in Pan, taking care of patients. One patient had been a tiny baby without arms and legs, and he'd somehow lost it in the tangled sheets. He woke in a mild panic, feeling it was real, but his numb hands and feet and the terrific pain in his neck and ankles brought him back to reality. Bard was nudging him with his foot.

"Up and at 'em, boy. Got to get going after we have a bite and some coffee."

"Jesus," said Jack.

Ismael was at the fire boiling water. It was daylight, but just barely.

Breakfast was canned tuna fish and grits, which made a mess in the pot. Ismael took a ragged pinecone and scrubbed the pot with stream water. With their gear loaded, they were on their way, headed now slightly southwest toward Laramore. Bard estimated it would take them about three hours of brisk hiking. They ascended the gap and passed through a grotto of jagged granite with scree underfoot, making them slip and slide. Jack warmed within fifteen minutes, and a light sweat coated the back of his neck. The trees were giants, mostly tulip poplars, some a hundred feet high. Leaves covered the ground, knee-deep in some places. The rhythmic swishing and crunching hypnotized Jack, and he imagined that he could hear voices in the cold wind. After an hour, a light rain fell, but they plowed ahead, intent on reaching a base of operations, a place where they could hide out for the next two weeks. The shadow of the dome at Laramore seemed the perfect place, thick with trees and pocketed with small caves.

They stopped to rest and drank from a tiny cold spring. Jack sank to the ground and closed his eyes. "Much farther?"

"Another hour," said Bard. "You can do it."

"How about that contact inside Laramore?" said Ismael. "Could be useful."

Bard cleaned his teeth with a twig from a young maple. "Yeah, might be able to slip us some victuals, some Scrumptious. He's a loner, which is good. He found us, though, on the radio, which makes me wonder if it's a setup."

"An Upright?" said Jack.

"Yeah, and Squad too. Hates the Infirm, from what I gather. Wants to join us, but I've hesitated to encourage him. If we get desperate, we'll have to take a chance with him."

"Does he know you're headed his way?" Jack picked up a stone and threw it at a tree.

"Nope," said Bard. "Talked with him about a week ago, before we found you." He stood, ready to move on. Sounds of the helicopter. "Well, shit, here they come again. Hug a tree." He hugged a fat chestnut oak.

Jack hugged a pignut hickory, and Ismael just squatted, pulling leaves over his dull blue backpack. The helicopter seemed to be flying a grid, passing them, fading away, and turning back, but never directly overhead. Jack had to pee. He looked at Bard hugging the tree and laughed. He imagined being tied to a tree and shot.

Above the rolling canopy, the pilot guided the copter in mile-wide swaths. With him were three Squad in full gear, ready to see some action or get home. It was alcohol day after all, and they had special privileges as Squad. One up front with the pilot of the twin-engine craft made of titanium craned his neck, looking out the window. In the back, the doors were open, the other two gazing down from either side. They were about frozen and wiped tears from their eyes. The Squad needed heat-seeking cameras, and an emergency request had been made to the feds.

"Anything?" said the pilot. He wore a thick, puffy flight suit and was quite toasty despite the cold.

"Nothing on this side," said his passenger. He wore an insulated Squad jumpsuit, camouflaged green and brown, with a SQUAD patch on the back. "See some deer running."

"Guys in the back?" said the pilot. "Haven't fallen out yet, have you?" He laughed into his microphone.

"Nada, nothing, maybe follow that creek?"

"We're in a pattern, Duke. Keep your eyes

peeled." The pilot had big front teeth like a rab-
bit. He reached the end of his line and banked left
to head back. "Whoa, what's that? Down in the
gap, rocks arranged. He dipped lower and swung
back. "Gonna land." The only place was uphill on
a sloped meadow. He brought it down nice and
slow, the rotor wash kicking up dirt and gravel. He
bumped it down and idled.

The two guys in the back, happy to be out of
their crouches, jumped down stiff-legged. This time,
they were armed with pistols and stun grenades.
They clattered down the layers of broken rock
and picked up a boot print here and there. Within
five minutes, they had located the rocks arranged
around a campfire.

"Has to be them," said one into his two-way radio. "Still some warm ash. Looks like they spent the
night here." He pulled out a tuna can and smelled it.

The two Squad lingered for a few minutes,
checking the perimeter, and then hiked back uphill.
It was decided that they should continue on foot,
while the copter continued reconnaissance. They
looked at each other like they'd been duped but
took off at a trot, glad to warm up.

~

Fifty-two saved his least favorite patient for last, before he had to make the rounds again. He could just
feel the whole dome getting sloshed one syringe at
a time. He had a buzz, taking sips here and there.
He scanned and knocked three times. The door
opened. He took a deep breath before laying eyes on
what he called the shit man. The smell hit him, and

he gagged.

The shit man was in bed, covered in his own shit. His large intestine had been routed to a stoma in the side of his neck. The shit came out there, usually liquid, and ran down his chest. His name was Frederick Langley, and he was somewhat of a cult figure. Other Infirm came to him for advice in spiritual matters. On his stomach and covered with feces was his big black Bible, which he was reading. He was forty-four, measured five-seven, and had short chestnut hair parted on the side. He also had leprosy and was missing his eyebrows and a few fingers. He only wore pants to let the shit stain his chest and dry in the hair there.

"Behold, the sinner approaches!" said Frederick. He shook his browned stubs at 52.

"Oh my," said 52. "Here I come, big daddy." He panted for breath, but that only made it worse. "Ready to get liquored up, oh sage of shitness."

"Watch your mouth, boy," said Frederick. "I will smite thee with a curse."

"You already have," said 52. "Okay, let's get this done."

"Alcohol is the devil's own sperm," said Frederick. "I forbid you!"

"Whatever," said 52. "Report me like you usually do. You know no one else will look after you but me. I'm all they've got. I guess we got each other." He laughed and choked, trying not to vomit. He would steal every last drop of Frederick's liquor and inject him with water instead. He wouldn't know the difference, but even acted drunk, as if the mere suggestion of alcohol inebriated him.

It was kind of like a game, and 52 made a huge show of pushing the water into Frederick's feeding tube. "Here she comes, you lush. You lost soul!" He had pocketed the real syringe and pushed water with a discard from another patient.

"Hell be damned, and you with it!" said Frederick. He arched back when the water hit his stomach as if in a great spasm of ecstasy. "Defiled again!" A gush of dark brown shit flowed down his neck and chest.

Fifty-two had to turn away and walk to the other side of the room. There was live video feed on the Chatty from the search for the Merry Woodsmen and Jack. A Squad in a jumpsuit was holding forth a small can as evidence. Fifty-two listened, ignoring the pleas and curses from Frederick. He would be meeting later that day with Kate and another Upright at 4:10 p.m., to hear about the latest radio transmission. He returned to Frederick and made a big show of the second syringe.

"Pure and straight from Satan himself, you bugger!" Fifty-two inserted the tip of the syringe into the feeding tube and pushed it long and slow. "Feel that, working through your veins, straight to that black brain of yours." For effect, he gave a wicked laugh.

Frederick sagged and raised his nubby hands in protest as if fighting a great battle. His eyes rolled in his head, and more shit came from his neck. He tried to speak, but nothing came, and he gasped, closing his eyes.

Fifty-two felt just a tiny bit bad and had to get

Frederick into his chair. It was the rule; otherwise, there would be bedsores, which were frowned on in most cases and punishable by fines of withheld Champy. He pushed the chair next to the bed and, as carefully as possible, slid Frederick over. He parked him in front of the Chatty and, as quickly as possible, washed his hands in the sink. He dry heaved once and rushed into the hall.

In a hurry, he made his second rounds, dosing the Infirm with their remaining syringes. Outside, he hurried to the shower, eager for a cleansing. The line was longer than usual, and he waited his turn, mumbling greetings, noticing that he would be showering with a couple of babes he admired. He disrobed, placed himself in the reclined cage, and was soon jerking along the conveyor through the hot water. He rubbed his face and hair, relishing the feeling of being clean. Once dry, he dressed in a crisp outfit of blue and stepped onto the street a new man. He checked the time projected on the dome. He had about half an hour to kill before his meeting. Not enough time to visit the museum, so he stepped into one of the mini-venues known as Jerry houses. Brightly lit, one could pay their respects there and watch screens of Jerry singing, bringing in the big bucks to promote muscular dystrophy, now the cornerstone Infirmity of the rich and famous or the few lucky enough to be born into it. Jerry's hair was slicked back with oil, glasses on, black suit with white shirt, the white cuffs shooting. The room was red, people sitting at tables. Jerry had a guest, a young doctor speaking to the advances in treating a variety of disorders related to MD. By discovering how to treat the disorder, it was discovered how to initiate the disorder. A genetic cure had been discovered in 2132 by a team of doctors in San Francisco, but very few had come forward for the cure, enamored by the status of the disease. Two successive presidents suffered from the malady, and then one with polio, reviving the memory of one of the icons of disability, Franklin Delano Roosevelt. Video of a little girl in a swing, talking about how sick her mommy had been.

Fifty-two dawdled, half watching the videos. He stood near a young woman who was also killing time, watching a smaller screen seeking volunteers to be infected with trachoma, an inversion of the eyelids that caused the lashes to scar the cornea, eventually leading to blindness. She scanned her ID to show that she was interested. Often, the Upright would dabble in a minor disability, testing the waters for possible conversion. He checked the time on the screen. Time to go.

He exited the venue onto the quiet street, and a few Upright were about, headed home or to the showers. He passed the Café Especial, headed for a Squad outpost a few blocks away. Beyond the dome, it was raining, a light hum and drum, the distant sound of thunder. The sodium lights were already on, casting an awful glare on the streets. Most of the Infirm were drunk or passed out in their flats, including the higher-ups, attended though by their personal helpers. Members of Squad were only an hour away from partaking in the day's festivities, just a skeleton crew to watch over the dome. He approached a bicycle rack. The other Upright was there, and she was a she. Mariah. Fifty-two pretended to look at a bicycle, clearing his throat. There was an alley where the cameras didn't reach. He ran his fingers over a smooth tire and made a face that said he would like to ride it.

Kate emerged from the single-story Squad building, wearing street clothes, but with her badge on a lanyard. Her forearms bristled, and she yelled at 52 to step away from the bikes.

Fifty-two held up his hands. "Sorry, ma'am." He turned and walked down the narrow alley filled with tidy trash bins.

"Hey, smart aleck, maybe we need to talk? And you, what are you looking at?" Kate told Mariah to get into the alley for questioning.

Mariah stammered and did as she was told, playing along. Just beyond the third trash bin, large and square, they gathered, Kate's hands on her hips, her finger wagging. She looked around, and all was clear.

"So, how goes the Merry Woodsmen and Jack?" said 52.

"Radio contact this morning," said Kate. "They're headed toward Laramore, hiding out there."

"How about Lura?" said Mariah. She was healthy, with long legs and a full head of blonde hair. Her smile came and went like a camera shutter.

"Still in the jail's general population. But the judge will be back in a few days. Her trial could happen any time. There's talk of a rescue, and possibly an uprising, us against them. If she's given death, there'll be hell to pay." She spat on the trash bin.

Fifty-two smiled. "Nothing like a lady in distress to get the ball rolling. Will the Woodsmen come back with Jack? Seems like he owes her."

Kate looked around for snoopers. "Yeah, they'll operate on the outside. We have to get Lura to them, probably through the sewer, unless we can spring an exit. Uh oh."

A spherical object the size of an orange, a hover-head, glided down the alley and stopped a few feet away, gathering data.

"Okay, you slackers! No more hanging around here, buckos! Back to the street before I take you in."

Fifty-two and Mariah backpedaled. "Yes, ma'am," said 52. "Sorry, ma'am. Just taking a shortcut." They entered the street and went their separate ways. The hover-head moved on.

Fifty-two didn't look back and walked the four blocks to his building. He had the syringes of alcohol tucked inside his waistband and longed for a drink. He entered 7800 and took the stairs to his room on the third floor, his graying hair tousled from the long day. He walked straight to the bin, and his Champy was there. He smiled. Champy and alcohol made a nice combo. The Chatty played a scene of a large lake with swans. He pulled out the syringes, which had cut into his belly, and sat on his small bed, the sheet in a wad. He kicked off his shoes and fingered the first syringe, a brown liquor. He took a squirt, swallowed, and winced, feeling the alcohol burn his throat. He thought about the shitman and laughed, then felt like crying. He was just so damn lonely, and tomorrow would start the cycle over again. He took another swallow and then another, relaxing onto his back, staring at the off-white ceiling and the light that never went off.

~

At the top of the next hill, the dome of Laramore rose in the distance through the trees, perhaps a mile away. "Thar she blows," said Bard. "There's a ridge just this way." He pointed. "Caves at the bottom, some with water."

Jack looked at his feet, expecting to just see nubs. "My ankles are screaming."

Bard laughed and motioned for them to follow. Within twenty minutes, a ridge of limestone lined with oaks loomed above them. They picked their way over and around rocks, soon reaching an oval opening close to the ground.

"We crawl in there, but first we need to gather wood for a fire," said Bard.

In silence, the three had no trouble gathering small limbs and shoving them into the crevice.

"I'll go in last," said Ismael. "Erase our tracks here."

Jack was the first in, crawling on his belly. Within five feet, the space opened up, and he stood, bumping his head. He could barely see in the darkness. Bard and Ismael followed.

"Cave goes back about twenty feet and branches off. This here is a good spot. Smoke from the fire mostly stays put, gathers on the ceiling, and leaks up through cracks." Bard had a handful of twigs, pine straw, and a weathered pinecone.

Ismael was the fire starter, and he had a small blaze going within a few minutes. Jack gazed around the room, about twenty feet high. He noticed a small pile of cans and bottles. He smelled urine. Water trickled down the wall to his left, pooling and running through a crack. The fire's light lapped at the shadows like yellow paint. He squatted on a rock and leaned against the cold, hard wall, closing his eyes, nodding off, and jerking awake.

"What's for dinner?" said Jack.

"Feeling puny?" Bard laughed, showing his big teeth.

"How about some more tuna mixed up with the Hamburger Helper. Three more boxes left and six cans. Says it's supposed to feed a family of four." Ismael fished through his backpack and arranged the items on the floor as if he were displaying jewelry.

Jack grunted his approval, fighting sleep. The Scrumptious kept you going for a whole day, but not this food from cans and boxes.

"Now look," said Bard. "They could be on our tail. We still need to keep watch. This cave leads to another. Have to climb through those two walls, another room up above, plus we can exit there and come out near the top of the ridge."

Cooling down, Jack zipped his coat and put on a knit hat that Ismael had given him. He watched Ismael methodically make the dinner, and his thoughts drifted to Lura, her short blonde hair, her ample breasts, and brown nipples. For months, they had been glancing at one another and making eye contact. He'd not had the nerve to speak to her, but had felt there was a mutual attraction. He'd known that she lived in 6200, but chancing on her room had been random, a stroke of luck perhaps.

Bard scratched his chest through his shirt and picked off burrs from his trousers, flicking them into the fire. "Tomorrow, radio contact. See what's going on back at Pan. Today was alcohol day, so the group should have been able to meet. But this whole thing could go bust at any time."

Ismael poured cold water into the pot and set it on to boil, then tackled the tuna can.

"Any of you guys ever been in love?" said Jack.

Bard took a seat on a rock. "Upright or Infirm?" He laughed.

"You know what I mean. Hadn't thought about falling in love with an Infirm. Too damn nasty, except for the crazy ones. Used to work on the south-side for a while. Had me a patient, a young lady who was bipolar and had seizures. She was a looker for sure."

"Yeah, you're right," said Bard. "I guess I had me a lady friend on the sly for a year or so. Name was Constance. I winked at her one day in the shower, and she winked back. We passed a few notes here and there, but never had the chance to shack up for a night. She made my bones hurt. Then, one day, she was just gone, transferred to another dome. I think they do that with the pretty ones, to keep 'em honest, to keep us fellas on the hook."

"Did you think about her?" said Jack. "I mean,

like every waking minute and sometimes dreams?"

Bard rubbed his jaw. "I still think about her. If I knew where she was, I might try and visit, stupid as it sounds."

"They could've taken her to make babies," said Ismael, stirring the pot.

"Yeah," said Bard.

Every state had its baby domes, where little ones were produced and raised. The female Uprights were artificially inseminated with Infirm seed. The Infirm infants were weeded from the Uprights and each sent to other domes to be raised. The Infirm babies were coddled and issued to various domes around the country at the age of twenty-one. The Uprights began their health training at fourteen and hit the ground running at sixteen, beginning their life's work as servants and caretakers.

"What about you, Ismael? Ever been in love?" said Jack.

Ismael stirred the pot. He'd dumped in the oily tuna fish. "Nope, not yet. Just trying to stay free. Nothing could ever come of it, so why try? So, I take it that you're in love?"

Jack opened his eyes. "Sad to say it, but I think I am, have been for a few months."

"With this Lura?" said Bard. "You sure do know how to show your love."

Jack cleared his throat. "Yeah, Lura. We could live in the wild. There's others like you out here, living on the outside, even having babies."

"Happens mostly out west, I hear," said Bard. "Domes are too close together here...Yeah, I'd like to have a child, maybe a son. I think about that quite a bit."

"Me too," said Jack. "I really owe Lura. If we can't be together, the least I can do is set her free."

"She could die out here," said Ismael. "Hate to say it. And I still don't understand how we haven't been caught. Like they're not really trying."

"We're pretty slippery," said Bard.

"You're like a legend on the inside," said Jack. "Maybe the Infirm let you roam to give the others some hope on the inside, something to think about."

"Well, that would be queer," said Bard. His breath smoked, and he wiped at his drippy nose. "But you can't really ever understand the Infirm."

"Guess not," said Jack. "If we get her free, I'd like to head south and see the ocean. I think she'd like that. Boats from other countries, maybe we could get on board and disappear."

"Well, you're a dreamer, boy," said Bard. "I'll live and die here, preferably on the outside."

"Bard, how old are you?" said Jack. The pot was cooling on the floor. He grabbed a bottle and held it under the water trickling from the ceiling.

"Forty-two. You?

"Thirty-three." The water burbled into the bottle.

"Twenty-four," said Ismael, "going on a hundred."

They talked until the pot was cool enough to pass around and ate their ration of Hamburger Helper, washed down with cold cave water.

~

Normally, Squad retreated to the dome at night-fall, but two from the helicopter had been dropped packs and ordered to continue the hunt. They had become utterly lost and settled in for a quick sleep just after the sun set. The moon would be out, giving them light to travel by. They hadn't bothered to pitch the tent and had bedded down near a mossy hole in the rock, beside a tiny spring.

Chad balled up in his sleeping bag, trying to stay warm. The ground was hard and smelled like dead leaves. "You think we can wake up?" Chad was tall and muscular, working out regularly in Squad's gym. He had a small soul patch on his chin.

"Heck, if we don't, what will it matter? No one's watching." Davies lay on his back looking at the stars through the trees. He was the youngest at eighteen and had big ears. His skin flushed easily, making his neck and face red most of the time.

"Well, what if they come across us in the night—"

"And shoot us in the kneecaps?" said Davies. He laughed, watching his breath float and disappear.

"Or in the head," said Chad. He closed his eyes, but they popped open. "Feel like a damn target lying here. But orders are to search through the night. That's all I know. Those guys are dangerous."

"And so are we," said Davies. "Let's get some shut-eye. If we wake up in a couple of hours, we'll move, but otherwise..."

"Oh, the confidence of youth," said Chad. "Damn, I can't sleep. There's no way." He scooted his bag against a tree and sat upright. "You sleep, baby girl, and I'll keep watch. Wake you in an hour or two."

"Whatever," said Davies, and soon he was snoring.

Chad listened to the night sounds, the wind through the trees, a sound of tinkling from the spring. He felt the pistol on his belt. The moon rose higher, and he imagined that whole weeks had passed. He checked his watch, and only fifteen minutes had gone by. He wondered if he should take his Champy, but he was ordered to abstain. He'd brought some anyway, but was afraid of the effects, worried that he wouldn't be able to defend himself. He looked ahead, and a ridge towered over them, dark holes pocketing the rock. He had to pee and cursed.

After ninety long minutes of Davies' snoring, Chad couldn't take it anymore. He crawled from his bag and nudged Davies with his foot. "Hey, let's move."

Davies gasped for breath and opened his eyes. "What the fuck?"

"Time to move on," said Chad. "Come on, we've got work to do. Let's find them before they find us."

"Christ," said Davies. "You're impossible." He stretched and yawned. "I suppose you'll report me, right?"

An owl passed overhead, its wings slicing the air. Chad crouched. "What the hell was that?"

"An owl, you dummy. Didn't you pay attention during briefing? They glide from tree to tree, hunting."

Chad stood. "Yeah, and we're supposed to be hunting too. Do you smell smoke?"

Davies sniffed the air. "Huh, maybe I do. That's not good." He sat up and looked around. Groaning, he unzipped his bag. "Damn, it's cold."

Chad held his finger to his lips. "Quiet. Let's just take a look around. Leave our stuff here. Then I'll let you get your beauty sleep."

Davies stood. He pointed to the ridgeline, and they walked that way, shivering, their boots crunching the leaves. "Lots of caves here. I guess you could have a fire in a cave." He was whispering, his eyes wide. "Come on."

They walked uphill a hundred feet or so and bore to the left, going another fifty feet.

"There," said Chad. He pointed toward the ground. There seemed to be dull light coming from within the base of the crumbling rock wall.

Davies pointed, and farther up the steep incline of rock, there was a wisp of smoke. "I'll be damned. A fire inside. They're in there." He gripped his pistol, a Lockmeyer.

They were both squatting, and Chad had to remember to breathe.

"Toss a grenade in there?" said Davies.

"Shit, not in the dark like this. They're trapped in there. Let's wait for sunrise." Chad was biting his nails.

"Okay, then. Might as well sleep, though. We'll keep watch." Davies retraced their steps back to their campsite with Chad in tow.

~

Friday, pet day and library day, Gretchen awoke, the Champy leaving her with a clean sleep. She checked the bin, removed the Scrumptious, and ate in small bites, watching the Chatty. It was the Great One. The text at the bottom revealed that his liver was failing, thus the yellowing skin. The purple light illuminating him helped metabolize the excess bilirubin in his blood. This was followed by a soothing voice announcing a promising diagnosis of autism, but that it would be two years before that diagnosis could be made, but all were praying. *I joined a gang of locusts, but failed to stomach their ideas!*

At the small sink, she washed her face and combed her hair into a ponytail, securing it with a rubber band. The Infirm made their pet choices known, but often it came down to the Uprights' preferences and what was available. In her district, the pets were kept on the first floor and basement of her shower facility. She walked two blocks to the big red S on the building. She had decided to check out a gecko for the day and just carry it from flat to flat, rather than bringing in new animals for each patient. Only the newbies did that.

Lizards were in the basement, and once there, she stood in the short line, waiting her turn. A small man with a bald spot was in front of her. He approached the counter and requested two kittens and a portable litter box. The man retrieving the animals looked tired, his face strained and red around his ears. He returned with two kittens, one black and one white, in a carrier.

"What'll do ya?" said the man. His name was

Jackson.

"Gecko, please. Mr. Winkles, if he's available." Gretchen especially liked Mr. Winkles. He took big steps with his gnarly legs and was patient, allowing himself to be stroked.

Jackson disappeared, then returned with Mr. Winkles in a small carrier. Already, he had crapped, making a small mess in there.

"Thanks, neighbor," said Gretchen. Jackson cracked a tiny smile.

Gretchen walked to 5400, and the scanner buzzed as she entered. She decided that Pearl Stillhouse would be the first visit of the day. On the main level, Gretchen knocked, scanning her ID. The door clicked open. She entered, and Pearl was on the toilet. She was able to maneuver herself around the flat, using the wheelchair and her muscular arms. She had no legs, suffered from cystic fibrosis, and had a hole between her ventricles. One could hear the heart murmur without a stethoscope.

"Hey, can you wipe me?" said Pearl. She coughed up a wad of phlegm and spat it between her legs into the commode.

Gretchen winced. "Sure. Got Mr. Winkles here." She placed the carrier on the floor, tended to Pearl's backside, then helped her transition to the chair.

"Oh, goody. Mr. Winkles," said Pearl. She rubbed her large hands together.

Gretchen glanced at the Chatty. It was breaking news as usual, about the search for Jack, "the Mutilator" as he was called. Apparently, Squad was hot on his trail, tracing him to the vicinity of Laramore.

She retrieved Mr. Winkles and held him up, admiring his delicate feet.

"Here you go," said Gretchen.

Pearl's body trembled as if she were chilled, and her chest rattled. A nurse came twice a day to hook her up to a vibropercussion machine to loosen the never-ending secretions in here lungs. She took Mr. Winkles and let him walk up her arm to her shoulder. "Oh, tickles."

Gretchen kept her ear to the Chatty, to a panel of experts debating the logic of Jack and his compatriots in their move toward Laramore. One went so far as to say that the Infirm of Laramore could be involved in a conspiracy to take over Pan. This brought sharp rebukes and laughter.

Mr. Winkles was climbing to the top of Pearl's bushy afro, clinging with his tiny feet, his eyes rotating like a doll's.

"Oh, Lord," said Pearl. "Don't let him mess in my hair. It's crazy enough as it is." And she did look a little off with her wild mound of hair.

Gretchen retrieved Mr. Winkles and placed him on Pearl's lap. Apparently, orders for Squad were to shoot first and ask questions later. They had been armed with guns, which was a rarity. Gretchen wondered what it was like to be shot. She knew that some Infirm underwent controlled shootings to non-vital portions of their bodies for style points.

"Had your Scrumptious?" said Gretchen.

"Yep," said Pearl. "I wonder what do Mr. Winkles eat?"

"Huh, I don't know," said Gretchen. She walked

around in a circle, checking the time on the Chatty. After thirty minutes, she told Pearl it was time to say goodbye to Mr. Winkles and placed him in his carrier.

"Goodbye, Mr. Winkles!" said Pearl, a tear in her bloodshot eyes.

Gretchen scanned out and headed to the next door. Inside, the room smelled of piss. Klaus Kugle's catheter bag had filled and ruptured during the night. He lay in bed, his face a mess of consternation.

"That you, Gretchen?" He suffered from retinitis and was nearly blind. His hands had been removed, and his ears trimmed. He looked like a little monster, and that's what Gretchen called him.

"Hey, little monster, you recovered from yesterday? Got Mr. Winkles here."

Klaus pushed up on his nubs. "Again? I told you I wanted to see a puppy dog. I want to pet a puppy dog." His voice croaked.

"Oh, I forgot," said Gretchen. "Next week we'll have a puppy, I promise. Let me get you cleaned up first." She threw back the sheet. The bed was soaked. She emptied the bag into the toilet and flushed, then stripped Karl. He shivered.

"Don't hurt me, please," said Klaus.

"Get you out of that mess. Come on and sit up." She maneuvered the wheelchair beside the bed and lifted him in, then stripped the bed and put on a clean sheet. She stuffed the dirty sheets into the laundry chute. Klaus sat there naked and trembling, waiting to be dressed, and she slipped him into a pair of clean pants and a shirt. "There, good as new."

"Thank you, Gretchen."

The Chatty was on the reproduction channel, showing baby after baby being born. One had a long cylindrical head, having been mashed to the shape of the birth canal.

"And now for Mr. Winkles."

"I don't want to hold him," said Klaus. "Just let me pet him."

Gretchen held Mr. Winkles and guided his nub there. Mr. Winkles rotated his eyes like he was going in two different directions and pumped air in his throat. The woman on screen was birthing standing up, and the baby dropped out like a bowling ball. Karl stroked Mr. Winkles with his nub, a tiny smile in the corners of his wet eyes.

Thirty minutes passed, and Gretchen gathered up Mr. Winkles, headed to the next patient, and after six hours, she was finished. She turned in Mr. Winkles, and it was time for her shower, which she looked forward to. Mr. Winkles had squirted poop on her blue uniform.

She joined the others, reclined in the rubberized steel cages, and relaxed, just letting the hot water and soap wash over her body as she clanked along through the circular shower. Dried and dressed, she had an hour to visit the library and hurried there. A big green L flashed on the building.

She wondered what book she would be given. It was a textbook of hydraulics filled with technical drawings and equations. She took her seat at a long wooden table filled with readers, all silent, except for two who were whispering. She perused the book, taking in what she could. There was a section on dams and the mechanism of power production, and then something called water hammer. Nothing really made sense, but she liked the way just sitting there surrounded by others made her feel.

Her hour passed quickly, and the lights flashed on and off. She closed the book and left it on the table, glancing at the woman beside her. She nodded. The woman nodded. She'd been reading a novel, *Barstool Babe*. Outside in the still air of the street, Gretchen meandered with the thin crowd of Uprights, headed back to her room. The woman who had been reading *Barstool Babe* came up right behind her, whispering.

"They're gonna execute Lura. Expect trouble. We need help with retaliation. You interested?" She was Mariah.

Gretchen slowed, gathering in the words. She knew what the woman was saying was true, and the execution would be unfair. She turned as if looking back down the street and met the woman's eyes, dark and fierce, her legs long, her hair brown. A smile flashed and then was gone. Gretchen hesitated. She knew that something was afoot.

"Count me in," said Gretchen. Her building was to her right, and she turned abruptly, leaving behind Mariah and her mysterious words. Something was coming together, and she would be part of it. A tingle crossed her face, and she touched herself there.

~

Bard was up first, washing his face in cold water straight from the cave floor. Ismael was at the entrance keeping watch. He had restarted the fire, which filled the top of the cave with smoke. Jack was awake, but with his eyes closed, trying to hold onto the warmth inside his coat.

Suddenly, something flew through the low opening of the cave. "Down!" yelled Bard. The stun grenade exploded, filling the chamber with a deafening roar. Jack reeled, rolled, and hit the far wall. The smell of burned gunpowder was overwhelming, and he gagged. Bard slumped with his back to the wall, a glazed look in his eyes. Ismael was the least injured, and he yelled for them to climb. "Go, go!" He was first to the narrow shaft and wedged himself in, pulling himself up to the cave above. Jack tried to stand, wavered, and nearly passed out. He shook Bard. "Have to go. Come on. Bard!" He slapped Bard, who mumbled. Jack pulled him up and pushed him toward the shaft, but Bard just stood there, swaying. Jack passed him and seemed to be lifted magically through the narrow opening. Ismael was pulling him up by the back of his coat. Jack collapsed, and Ismael yelled down for Bard.

Bard blinked and gathered his marbles. He wedged himself in the crack and pushed himself up, crawling over the lip into the chamber. From there was a passage that led up farther still to an opening just below the ridgeline. A path led up from there. Ismael was already at the exit, waiting for Jack and Bard. It took a minute, but soon all three were gathered. He held his finger to his lips, his ears ringing.

"Wait till we hear voices, then we head out and up."

Outside the cave, Davies and Chad crouched, waiting. "We have to go in," said Davies. His face and neck were flushed. "I'll go first, and then you."

"Let's wait for another minute," said Chad. "They're trapped. Damn, that was loud."

"Yeah, but they're stunned. They'll recover. I'm going in." Davies dropped to his belly, his pistol in his hand. He scooted through the opening and came up quickly, pointing his Lockmeyer around the dim room. The room was still clouded with smoke. The grenade had landed in the fire and blown it to pieces. There was no one, and he heard Chad scrambling inside. "Nothing. What the hell?"

They stood there, guns drawn. "The hell," said Chad. He peered around the cave, the water trickling from above, and noticed the narrow shaft. "Maybe they went up?"

Davies' heart was in his mouth. He'd been expecting a gun battle. "Could be. Let's see. But maybe you go back out. They could be getting away."

"Right," said Chad. He went to his belly and crawled out.

Bard and Jack followed Ismael, still in shock. They exited the cave, looked down, then up. One slip and it was a thirty-foot fall. Ismael turned, encouraging them. He scrambled up, using his hands and feet until he was at the top. Dazed, Jack and Bard followed. Without hesitating, Ismael slung the rifle onto his back and broke into a run, heading into the woods away from the ridgeline. He could hear the crashing of leaves behind him.

Outside the cave, Chad scanned the rock face but saw nothing. He swiveled and looked back toward the campsite. They would have to leave their things there and move. He heard a voice calling his name and looked up. Davies was standing in a narrow opening up above, motioning for him to follow.

"Shit," said Chad, and he began the torturous climb of the rock face. He slipped and had to jump back down ten feet, turning his ankle. "Dammit." He tried another route and was soon even with Davies.

"They had to go up," said Davies. "Let's move. We should have called in the helicopter. No time now." He noticed boot prints in the leaves of the rocky chute. He went first, clambering upward, his chest tight with adrenaline.

At the top, they stood there, gazing in all directions.

"There," said Chad. A ragged line in the upturned leaves.

They took off.

The Merry Woodsmen tore through the forest like frightened deer, running down slippery hillocks and then trudging as fast as they could uphill. They came to a small creek, and Ismael stopped. "Walk in the creek, this way." He turned toward what he imagined was away from Laramore. The three stepped over the rocks and through the cold water, trying not to fall. They'd had to leave their packs and had no food.

For ten minutes, they walked in the creek, and then Ismael stepped out, headed due north, steam streaming from his mouth. Briefly, they stopped to listen and heard nothing, and continued for nearly an hour before dropping from exhaustion inside a thick stand of cedar.

Jack said, "Good God," panting and wheezing.

"I think we shook 'em," said Bard. His hair looked wild, as if he had taken the force of the grenade to his face. He was on his knees.

Ismael took deep breaths. "Well, that was exciting. They could still be on our trail, though. I say we walk until dark. There's an old cabin somewhere north of here. Some supplies there."

"Good idea," said Bard. He groaned and led the way, keeping his eyes open for an old trail that led to the cabin.

Having lost the trail, Chad and Davies stopped to rest.

"Need to head back and call in the helicopter," said Chad. "No use getting lost." He bent over, catching his breath.

"Damn," said Davies. "We had them. Central's not going to like this."

"Central can go to hell," said Chad.

"Probably so," said Chad. "So, come on."

It took them forty-five minutes to retrace their path and reach the ridgeline. Down they went, slipping and sliding, soon reaching their gear and radio. Chad called in the report and listened incredulously as the Squad captain ordered them to continue pursuit. The helicopter would arrive within half an hour.

"Ugh," said Davies. "Well, those are orders, I guess. Let's give it another try. I'd say split up, but that's too dangerous, I think."

"Hell, we can take a break, though. Need to eat and drink."

They sat, leaning against pine trees, eating their Scrumptious and drinking water. Soon, they were ready and set off again in hot pursuit.

Bard was taking them on a wide zigzag path to pick up the trail. When he saw the ancient wreckage of a small plane, just scraps of white aluminum, he knew they were in the vicinity and adjusted his course. Jack was lagging, and their pace slowed because of him, but it was Jack who pointed out the trail, his eyes cast downward as he trudged along.

"Good eyes, boy," said Bard. He slapped Jack on the back.

The trail was narrow and overgrown, barely a path, and they followed it for another hour. The sun was high overhead, beginning its descent toward the west. The day had warmed to nearly fifty degrees, and all three had removed their coats. They had not encountered any water, and the three were thirsty, licking their dry lips.

"Yo!" said Bard. The cabin made of oak logs was just ahead. "Home sweet home."

Jack surveyed the small building. It looked like a dump, trees growing around it. Part of the wood-shingled roof was missing.

Ismael took the lead and swung back the rotting door. Inside was a shambles, as if a bear had ravaged it, and one had. An old cast-iron stove stood in the middle of the single room, shelving crashed to the floor, cans dented, boxes destroyed.

"There's a spring just down the hill," said Bard. "We need water." There was an empty can, and he took it. Ismael and Jack followed, eager to drink. Once filled with cold spring water, they were back at the cabin, examining the cans, many without labels.

"I am sorely hungry," said Bard.

Ismael took a pocketknife and attacked a can. He pierced the top and smelled. "Some kind of vegetable." He worked the can with his knife and peeled back the lid. "Beans!" He held the can to his mouth and let the white beans slide in. "Damn, that's good." He handed the can to Bard, and then Jack took a turn while Ismael was tackling another can, which was more beans.

Filled with beans, the three collapsed and leaned against the rough log walls.

"Think we're safe here?" said Jack.

"Oh hell, they don't even know this cabin exists, I guarantee you. Never knew about it when I was Squad. Damn, my ears still ringing from that damn grenade."

"You were pretty out of it," said Jack.

"Still am," said Bard.

"Fire in the stove?" said Ismael. "Might warm this place up a bit."

"Yeah, I've been hot all day, but I can tell I'm going to freeze my ass off tonight." Jack pulled on his knit hat and zipped his coat.

"Important thing is to rest," said Bard. "They'll

be hot on us tomorrow, no doubt. You hear that?"

"Yeah, helicopter," said Jack.

Ismael ran back inside with a few arm-sized branches. "They're looking for sure. No fire for a while."

"So, you still in love?" said Bard. "This is just the tip of the iceberg, compared to what's coming."

Jack sighed, thinking of Lura. She should be in the showers about now, others ogling her body. It was common for an Upright to masturbate there, getting a quick rinse in the process. "I don't know. If you mean is this worth it, I'd say yes. I'm pretty set on getting her out of there. What happens after that is anybody's guess."

"Well, here's hoping," said Bard. "We could use us a lady, if she's fit and suited for the moving around. Right now, Ismael is my wife, cooking for me." He laughed.

"I want a fur coat and some new dishes, big daddy," said Ismael. He was breaking the limbs into smaller pieces. The helicopter droned, sweeping the area. There was so much growth around the cabin that it was hard to see.

"Yeah, old Ismael makes a good wife," said Bard.

"Is it really true that people used to live together?" said Jack. "Seems weird. To share a room with someone."

"Yeah, they used to get married, a legal bond, and have kids and raise them. Some of them Jerry Lewis videos show families with kids. Lived in big houses. You can still find foundations here and there."

"There's a few in the dome, near the park," said Ismael. He arranged kindling inside the stove.

"I guess those were the good old days," said Jack. "Wonder why it faded away?"

"Well, these damned Infirm did away with marriage. Not sure why, except to keep a tighter rein. If you have a family, what's the point of being a slave? Seems like you'd fight for yourself and the Infirm be damned."

"Makes sense," said Jack. He staggered up and stretched. Above him was a hole in the roof about the size of a torso. The rest sagged. "Wish we could cover that damn hole."

The helicopter was approaching again and passed directly overhead.

"Right under their noses," said Bard. He licked his big yellow teeth. "But we lost our radio. No doubt they took it."

They paced inside the cabin, the chopping noise of the helicopter growing farther away. They decided it was safe to build a fire, and Ismael had it going within minutes. He placed a couple of branches over the sticks, but left the stove door open. The vent pipe was separated at the ceiling, and smoke filled the room at chest level, so everyone sat down. In the distance, an owl hooted, and a pall of sleep overcame the trio.

~

Saturday dawned bright and cheerless, frost on the lower reaches of the dome. Fifty-two ate and washed his face, headed out for game day. All the Infirm kept a pack of cards in their flats along with dice. It was also smoking day, which was encouraged. Lung cancer had been all the rage a few decades prior, but had fallen somewhat out of favor.

Fifty-two headed toward his assigned building, 6200. He wanted to catch the news on a Chatty and decided to visit old Peters first. He always had the news on. He knocked and scanned. He pushed the door in, and there was Sammy Peters, already shuffling the cards.

"Gonna beat your ass, boy," said Peters. He'd had his lips trimmed off, and his teeth looked like weapons. Otherwise, his head was shaped like an olive. He'd had his knees removed as a result of severe arthritis and couldn't walk. He liked to bend his foot up to his mouth and gnaw on the nails. He was due for an invasive surgery to route his spleen to his chest. He was sweet on an old lady down the hall who was always calling him a pussy, and he was determined to impress her.

Fifty-two checked the bin and removed the Scrumptious, handing it to the old man, then fetched a glass of water. The Chatty played the news, the volume cranked. He listened to the breaking news, first the story of a shower incident. Three Uprights had been scalded accidentally. A panel of experts was weighing the pros and cons of a good old-fashioned scalding.

"If it's third-degree burns, I say they be given the option to convert to our side," said a grumpy dwarf. He'd had his fingers removed and his big toes transplanted to the ends of his hands. They kind of looked like erect penises.

"Well, we'd have people scalding themselves on purpose. There's a shortage of good-quality Uprights as it is," said a scowling woman with a horrific red birthmark on her face. She had a glioma in her brain that gave her headaches, made her face twitch, and that pulsed a burning down her left side.

Fifty-two turned his attention back to Peters, who was still munching his Scrumptious, which caked his exposed teeth. His lower legs were all askew with his missing knees. "Sit at the table, in your chair?"

Peters swallowed. He looked like a cartoon. "Yeah, sure, gonna whoop your ass, boy. Canasta. Caaahnaasta!"

"Hell, we'll need two decks. You got two decks?" He helped Peters slide into his chair.

"Oh yeah, got me four, two new ones dropped in the bin this morning. The glass of water sitting on his bed fell over, soaking his sheets. "Well, shazam!"

Fifty-two laughed, listening to the Chatty, but trying not to look. These panels of experts bored the hell out of him. Just give the damn news. No need to reflect, for god's sake. The Infirm were so damn reflective.

Peters dealt the cards, two hands of eleven cards each. "You know any of them Uprights got scalded in the shower?"

"Other side of town, so no," said 52. He gazed at his cards, trying to remember the rules, which were something like rummy.

"Some say they were targeted, punished," said

Peters. "Rumor has it they were having sex in the alley, but couldn't catch 'em. They took down one of the hover-heads and smashed it to pieces. They were scalded on purpose."

"Huh," said 52. The expert panel was interrupted by breaking news. This time it was the Merry Woodsmen. "Hold up, I want to hear this."

The video anchor had two heads, one alive and well, and the other puny and drawn. They were reading off a prompter.

The healthy head spoke in a deep voice. "Squad made contact early this morning with the escapees, including Jack. He has taken the Merry Woodsmen in full allegiance, punishable by death."

The screen switched to a rough view of two Squad, Davies and Chad. They explained how they waited till morning and threw a stun grenade into the cave, but the felons had escaped through a getaway shaft in the cave. They had tried to follow but lost them in the thick woods. They had seemed to be heading to Laramore, raising suspicion that the dome there was somehow in cahoots. Both then gave sincere apologies to the Great One and the judge, Chet Spurlock, who was recovering nicely from his surgical adventure.

Fifty-two wondered where they could be. They couldn't hide forever, or could they? He turned back to Peters as a new panel of experts appeared, including Cornelius Fava of Central. His voice was distinctive, like a polished recording.

Peters was eyeing his cards, pairing them up. He had two jokers and two wild twos. "You know that scoundrel, Jack? He's in for it."

Fifty-two nodded his head. "Seen him around. Seemed like a decent guy. Must have just gone nuts. I sure would hate to be him."

"That judge'll string him up for sure. Hearsay is he'll be castrated and then hanged." He chuckled. "I'd like to see that, the bastard. Right? Am I right?"

"Yeah, right," said 52. "But that'll be one less. Who's gonna play cards with you bastards if we keep getting bumped off?"

"Watch your tongue," said Peters. "I'll report you." He nodded his olive head, the hair falling just to his eyebrows. He licked his dry teeth.

"Take it easy. We're buds, you and me. Right. Where's your sense of humor?"

Peters busily arranged his cards. "Wanna put something on it?"

Fifty-two could see it coming. "I think not. Sex day is all you get."

Peters frowned. "Well then, how about we play for Champy? I like what you brung me last time. Had me a wild time."

"Can't do it. I need it to get through the night. The long, long night," said 52. He briefly took stock of his life and found it severely wanting.

Peters drew a card from the deck, hesitated, and then put a card in the discard pile.

"So, what about this Lura. What have you heard?" said 52.

"She's in hot water, for sure. The Chatty says she's been arraigned. Just waiting on the old judge to size her up. I expect they'll hang her along with that Jack fellow. You gonna play cards or just talk? This is game day, boy," said Peters.

"Yeah, right." Fifty-two took a card. He'd felt up to it, but the life seemed to be drained from his body. He needed a change and bad. He was hinging his hopes on an uprising, not caring if he actually survived it. He imagined himself being hanged. He stared at his cards, wishing them just to disappear. "Can't do it, today, old man. I fold. You win."

"What? You're sworn to it. You have to play. What's got you so down in the mouth?"

He sighed. "Look, my brain just can't do it today. Why can't you pick something simpler, like twenty-one or even poker? Canasta? Why don't we just go and smoke? I could really use a smoke." He dropped his cards on the small round table and leaned back in the tiny chair.

"I'll let you win. That what you're afraid of, getting your tail beat?"

"No," said 52, and he lightly hammered the table. "Need some tobacco."

"Well, hell then. Have it your damn way. I'll have to report you, though. I like game day."

"Of course you do. Otherwise, you're just rotting away inside this room. What are you gonna do next, have them cut off your ears?"

"Well, I've thought about it. If it can get me some pussy, I sure will. Got me a girlfriend down the hall, though she don't know it."

"Hell, that wench. Her boobs lay in her lap like some kind of vegetables." The thought of Anabell Winsome made him cringe. Her privates were a mess, like a tangle of rubber bands down there.

"Hey, don't be bad mouthing my missy. What's gotten into you, boy?"

"What do you think my life is like? I don't have a life, and neither do you. It's like we suck on each other, suck the life out of each other, except you get to call the shots. It's fucking ridiculous."

Peters frowned. "Maybe you do need a smoke."

Fifty-two laughed. He heard a thump in the bin and went to check.

~

Lura sat up straight, her hair brushing the ceiling. "What the hell?" Gomer was raking his baton across the bars, making a tremendous racket.

"Judgment day!" said Gomer.

"Get the hell away from here!" said Mae. She groaned, thinking about what she would have to do to get more Champy.

"The judge is out of the hospital with his new steel dick and rubber balls," said Gomer. "Time to pay the piper."

"What? When?" said Lura. "There has to be a trial, right?"

Gomer laughed and pushed out his big belly. "He'll do with you as he pleases. You've got thirty minutes to gather your scattered brains. He wants you on the Chatty."

"Good god, motherfuck," said Mae. "You can't be serious." She looked pouty with her big red lips.

"Hell," said Lura. She just about heaved.

"Oh, baby doll, I'm sorry," said Mae, from her back. "Maybe he just wants to give you a good tongue lashing, is all."

Lura slid off the bunk, sat on the toilet, and peed. She stared at Gomer through the bars. She rinsed her hands and checked the bin, but then felt nauseated at the thought of eating. Where was Jack, her knight in shining armor?

"Can't believe it, can't fucking believe it," said Lura. "I didn't do a damn thing. I couldn't. I was high as a kite."

Mae was up, put her arm around Lura, and gave her a big smile. "He'll know all that. He'll go easy on you. Probably just wants to put the fear into you, is all."

Gomer clucked his tongue and walked away down the hall.

Lura was shaking. "Thanks, Mae. Maybe so." She broke away and held to the cold bars. On the Chatty, there was a long shot of the Great One superimposed against a background of swirling psychedelic colors. *I gave her CPR, but her lungs were in her mouth!* She pulled on the bars as if she could bend them and began to cry.

Mae tried to drape an arm over, but Lura shrugged her off. "I just won't leave the cell."

"I wouldn't try that. They have ways. Make it easy on yourself. Take a bite of breakfast, settle your stomach, drink some water. Pretend like it's just another day. When you see him, just realize him for what he is, a bastard who deserved what he got. Be strong. You can do it. Here, sit on my bunk."

Lura sat and nibbled at the chunk of Scrumptious. She imagined it tasted like blood when you cut your finger and sucked on it. She fought to swallow and had to get a cup of water. "Why me?"

Mae did her best to comfort her, but Lura climbed back on her bunk, ready to resist being extracted from the cell. She lay on her side, facing the off-white wall, waiting. Time seemed to stop, and she imagined that hours had passed when she heard Gomer calling for her to back up to the bars to get cuffed. She ignored him.

"Hey, get your ass over here, pronto! That's an order," said Gomer.

"Bite me!" said Lura.

"Lord," said Mae. "Just come on down, honey. It'll just be the Chatty. He won't really be there."

Gomer saw what was what and pulled the radio from his belt, calling for help. "Got a struggle bunny in fourteen on two. Need two officers."

Within minutes, two more guards appeared, one male and one female. They kind of looked like Gomer, as if that was a job requirement.

"One last call, young lady," said Gomer. "Get your ass down here."

Lura stared at the wall, a surge of adrenaline wiring her body. She heard the cell door open. Mae was escorted into the hall. "Don't get hurt, now, babydoll," she said.

Gomer and the other male guard entered the cell, walking slowly. Without speaking, Gomer reached and grabbed her legs and pulled. Lura sprang open like a safety pin, kicking and thrashing. Gomer stumbled backwards, but with the other guard, the pair wrestled her down and pinned her to the floor. Gomer was panting and cursing. She'd torn his shirt and caused his stun gun to fall off his belt. The other guard cuffed her, and together they pulled her up, her hair a mess, her lower lip busted and bleeding into her mouth.

"Bastards," said Lura, and she was shoved into the hallway and led to the locked door, which clanked open. Gomer used his key to open the other lock.

Gomer and his accomplice ushered her through the second block, then pushed Lura into a small room and made her sit in a chair, with one standing on either side of her. The Chatty was fuzzy.

"Reckoning day, missy," said Gomer. "Try anything, and we'll stun you long and hard. Got it?"

Lura swallowed blood, staring at the blank screen.

The Chatty seemed to glitch, and there were snatches of a face that soon melded into that of the Judge Spurlock. He was visible from the shoulders up and appeared to be in his flat with an Upright hovering behind him. The judge had an eager but somber look on his face, his lazy eye wandering like a lost sheep. Lura stared straight ahead, focusing on the judge's neck.

"Well, hello, gentlemen, and the lady. Such a pretty thing. No wonder Jack chose you as his accomplice." He cocooned his chin into his lobster-claw hands. His sandy hair, splotched with gray, was neatly combed on his high forehead.

"I'm innocent," said Lura. "He kidnapped me."

"Yes, well, we'll add that to his list of charges.

How about that? Feel better some?"

Lura strained against her cuffs, which were digging into her back. "Whatever."

"You do know the punishment for being an accomplice in a case such as this, correct?"

"Hell, how would I know?" said Lura. "I'm innocent."

"You tried to escape with him, down the sewer, but you were too slow, am I correct?"

"No, you're not correct," said Lura. She gathered the courage to look the judge in the eye and was surprised. Except for the lazy eye, it was the fat and puffy face of a baby.

"You're lovers, you two, am I right?" said the judge. "Star-crossed lovers, it seems. Romeo and Juliet. Do you know the story? Have you read it on library day? You know we do all of these nice things for you people, and all you do is rebel. Why is that?"

"You think an hour in a library is something? We're basically slaves, except we get to go home at the end of the day." Lura drew herself up and looked the judge in the eyes.

"Yes, well, it's your lot in life. You have to accept that. But now you've gone and done a terrible thing to your keepers. You must and will be punished."

At that, Lura's voice caught, and she swallowed hard. "I have the right to a trial, sir."

"You have the right to one hour in the library," said the judge. "For now, let's rest and reflect. We'll have this settled in due time and perhaps the Merry Woodsmen as well. There's no hurry, is there, dear Lura? Dear sweet Lura." His face cracked a smile.

"Go to hell," said Lura, her voice shrill.

"Yes, but after you..." and the screen faded to snow and then to the Great One, a great gob of drool on his lips. *Picking up twigs that look like nails.*

~

They hadn't kept watch that night, and all three awoke, aching but rested. There were coals still in the stove, and Ismael rekindled the fire. Bard groped through the mess of cans on the floor and chose two large ones without labels. The first can was hominy, and the second was pinto beans. Without fanfare, the cans made the rounds and soon were empty. Their next item of business was water, and they exited the cabin, headed to the nearby spring, gazing about, looking up through the tangle of leafless oaks, maple, and hickory. The day was cold, the sky overcast with low clouds of gray. They slurped at the cold spring water until they sloshed.

"Well, no radio," said Bard. He belched. "So, no contact with Laramore or with the team back in Pan."

"We're S-O-L," said Ismael. "We need more supplies. Can't go back to the cave."

"Don't be such a Debbie Downer," said Bard.

"You started it with the radio bit," said Ismael.

"Indeed, you did," said Jack.

"Okay, whatever," said Bard.

They walked uphill to the cabin, leaves and twigs crunching beneath their boots. There was a broad stoop of rocks, and they sat there in the dull sunlight.

Jack spoke. "You think those guys headed back

to the cave? They could still be on our trail, unless the helicopter took them out."

"My guess is they flew out, but knowing the Infirm, they could have been ordered to camp out and resume the search, which would be about now."

"So, where do we go from here?" said Jack. "It's like we're playing hopscotch." He'd read about hopscotch in the library.

"Hopscotch?" said Bard.

"Oh, it's a game kids used to play," said Jack.

"Well," said Bard. "We can stay put and hope they miss us. I say we go farther north and then loop back toward Pan. There's a canyon with big rock rooms behind waterfalls. We'd be hard to find there, although we could get trapped."

"Anymore wamas?" said Jack.

"Not that I know of. Most were razed to the ground. There's an occasional old store and what used to be gas stations. We could make good time on some of the roads, but we'd be too exposed, although most have been overcome with jungle."

"Huh, jungle. That's a strange word," said Ismael. "Jungle, jingle, jangle." He scraped his boot with a stick.

Chad and Davies had spent the night at their camp below the caves. They had been on the verge of cold all night, never getting warm. The helicopter would be back to resupply them and perhaps drop them farther north, their best guess unless the trio had somehow infiltrated Laramore.

Chad groaned and crawled out of his sleeping

bag. He stretched, flexing his muscular arms, and scratched his soul patch. "Get up, you lazy whore." He reached into his pack for some Scrumptious and chewed the dry chunks, making a face.

Davies cursed him and unzipped his bag. "Could've waited till the helicopter gets here."

"Damn helicopter," said Chad. "How come we get stuck with this? How about some of the other guys helping out? Let them sleep outside for God's sake."

"Because we're beautiful people, I suppose," said Davies. "Wanna smoke? At least we got that. Today's smoking day."

"Yeah, I was thinking about that. What do we have?"

Davies reached into his silver pack and pulled out a padded envelope with six cigars. "Imported from Honduras. Looks good, a dark wrapper. That's about like getting a shot in the arm." He handed Chad a cigar. The band said Punch.

"Like a punch to the gut." He waited for Davies to bite the end off and light up, then took the butane lighter. He puffed and sent out a cloud of gray-white smoke. "Ahh, that's the trick."

They leaned against pine trees, smoking, waiting for something to happen. They could hear the helicopter in the distance, a sound like a blade going through a bag of rice. There was no place to land nearby, and they stood waving their arms, Chad on his two-way radio.

"We see ya, good buddy. Over," said the pilot. He hovered the craft about fifty feet above the trees.

A Squad in the cargo area took the two packs laden with a week's worth of supplies and more stun grenades and lowered them through the trees.

"Give us the good stuff," said Chad. "Any alcohol in there? Over."

"Alcohol day is Thursday," said the pilot. "This is fucking Saturday. Over." He laughed.

"Yeah, fuck you too," said Chad. He shook his fist at the sky.

The packs hit the ground, and Davies released the cable and saluted.

"We're gonna do recon further north," said the pilot. "Should have enough fuel for a three-hour search. Will keep you posted. Over."

"Yeah, right," said Chad. "We're freezing our asses off out here. Over."

"More power to ya. Over and out," said the pilot as he ascended, tilted down, and headed off into the wild blue yonder.

"Well, damn, these packs weigh a ton," said Davies. His face and neck were flushed red.

"Feel like a damn mule." Chad squinted at the morning sun.

They broke camp, leaving their smaller packs behind, and filled their water bottles from the cave stream. First thing was ascending the steep rock wall, and they climbed up cursing one another and their superiors. They followed their earlier path until reaching the stream, where they had lost the evidence of boots trouncing and scattered leaves. It had taken them over two hours. The helicopter came within earshot on two occasions, but there was no radio contact, which meant no developments.

"So, they must have walked in the creek to throw us off," said Davies. "But which way to go?"

"Well, let's try west," said Chad. "We'll go for a mile or so."

"Okay," said Davies, walking along the rocky bank of the small creek. He could see minnows flitting in response to his shadow. "You know they could have doubled back."

"Just pray that the damn copter finds them. Looks like they think we'll spend the whole week out here," said Chad. "Hell, they could be in another cave for all we know. We just got lucky."

They walked for over a mile, seeing nothing except scrub, briars, rocks, some robins in a clearing, and an old rusted barrel. They tried the two-way radio, but there was no response. Tired, they turned back, headed east to try and pick up evidence of boots. They each smoked a fat cigar as they walked. They soon reached the starting point and continued, walking beside the babbling creek filled with cold, clear water. Within twenty minutes, they had made another mile and stopped.

"Hell, we missed 'em," said Chad.

"Well, I say we just go north from here. The map shows some old roads. Could be buildings. At least we could sleep inside tonight. Who knows, we might stumble across them. We just might." Davies patted the pistol on his belt.

"I need to loosen up my back and shoulders. This pack's a humdinger." Chad let the pack to the ground, dropped, and did fifty pushups without much effort. He stood and stretched.

"Well, that was fun," said Davies. "Let's hit it," and he led the way up a gentle slope that steepened as they walked, forcing them into a zigzag.

The trio marched along in single file, occasionally getting tangled in briars and skirting downed trees. All three noted that it was smoking day and rued their lack of tobacco. The tobacco at the wama had long since disappeared, although there had been lighters. Bard broke into an old Army song. "I know a girl who's plumb out of luck! She likes ice cream, and she sure likes to fuck!"

"Did you hear that at the library?" said Ismael.

"Yep, from World War Three, Chinese and Russians versus the United States and Europe. Bloody hell, it was."

"That was over three hundred years ago," said Jack.

"First war we actually fought here," said Bard. "Goddamned nuclear shit. No wonder there's so many defectives."

They reached the top of a ridge that for half a mile led to a small canyon. Down they went, zigging and zagging to keep from tumbling. At the bottom was a wide creek, the banks flooded with rhododendron and some large magnolias. The scene looked ancient. They stopped to drink, and Ismael produced a surprise granola bar, which they shared.

Without a pack, Jack's ankles were faring better, but the raw blisters on his feet hurt like hell. He poured the granola into his mouth. "Kind of like

Scrumptious but with actual flavor."

"Yeah, sometimes I miss it," said Bard. "Real filling. You can say that."

"But what's in it?" said Jack. "The Scrumptious."

Ismael spoke. "Mostly corn, from what I know, but nothing goes to waste in the dome. So, people speculate."

"Could be the dead in there for all we know," said Bard.

"Thought maybe you'd know since you were Squad." Jack scratched his oily head.

"They don't tell us squat," said Bard. "Just get privileges, like tobacco and regular Champy."

"I could sure use a wallop of Champy," said Jack. "I think I'm in withdrawal. Feel shaky at night without it."

"Well, girls, shall we go? No time to waste. There'll be more of these little canyons until we reach the biggest." Bard had pulled out his pocket-knife and was trimming his nails.

They continued, their pace slowed by the steep ups and downs. They came to an area filled with cement and stone foundations, a network of roads covered with soil and smaller trees.

"Here's one with a basement," said Bard. "Let's take a look-see."

Cement stairs led beneath a floor of reinforced concrete. The steps down were layered in dirt and lichen. Jack was last, breathing in the dank mushroom air. His eyes adjusted. Steel support poles. An ancient bicycle, old cans. The sound of the helicopter. Jack felt the need to run.

"We're safe down here. Look," said Bard. "That's an old washing machine and a dryer." He opened the dryer door, and it fell off. Inside were rotting clothes. He pulled out an old pair of what looked to be pants and held them up.

"What's this?" said Jack. He picked up a rusted rifle with a large bore.

"That's an old-timey shotgun, uses shells. Wish we had some shells. Might still work. There was a rusted steel table with cabinets, and Bard opened one. It was empty except for a few small screws. "This could be a good place to hide out."

"Maybe not," said Ismael. "Let's get to the canyon. No water here."

Bard grunted in agreement. "Well then, let's get going. No use wasting time. Just wanted to see if there was anything useful." He kicked a screwdriver.

Back outside, the helicopter gone, a light rain was falling.

"Hell, we'll catch pneumonia," said Jack. He adjusted his knit hat, his toboggan, as he knew it.

On they trudged, passing through a small stand of umbrella magnolias. They crossed another deep canyon, filled up on water, and continued for another hour, meandering north, cutting slanted paths up the thickly forested hillsides, soon reaching the big canyon. The walk down was steep, but not as steep as the smaller canyons. All of a sudden, an intact bridge made of steel and cement appeared. A large creek, or was it a small river, flowed beneath the bridge.

"That's it, we're here," said Bard. "Just need to

follow the water upstream. About five miles, there's a pocket canyon."

"I hate to say this," said Jack. "But what will we eat?"

"Whatever we can find, brother," said Bard. "Mushrooms, berries, nuts, bugs, if we have to. No wama out here."

"Haven't really seen any bugs," said Jack. "You can eat bugs?"

"Hell, yeah," said Bard. "They'll never look where they think there's no food." He motioned for them to follow, and they descended to the bridge, admiring the handiwork. The creek looked deep in places, about twenty feet across, and flowing with a cool rush.

They kept close to the water, following it as it curved. Gradually, walls of limestone gathered on their right with a steep uphill climb through trees on the far bank. Rainwater dripped from the recent shower, and all three shivered as cool air rose from the creek.

"Feels like the AC is on," said Jack. "Hold up." He stooped, shaking, and tied a loose lace.

It took them two hours, but they reached a tight bend in the creek where a lively stream plunged, surrounded by giant tulip poplars and beech trees.

"Ismael, help me out. Head thisaway?" Bard pointed.

Ismael nodded. "Think so."

The ground climbed at first and then leveled. Boulders slowed them down. Ten minutes later, the area opened, filled with tulip poplars that it would take two men to reach around. Just beyond the open area, they followed the stream into an ancient, narrow canyon. And just beyond that was a half-circle cliff with a fifty-foot waterfall, a slender, continuous stream of water that splashed into a clear pool.

"Sure is pretty," said Bard.

"Wow," said Jack. "I feel like I've been swallowed by nature."

"Behind that waterfall, it's hollowed out, nice and dry."

Jack sat on a log, exhausted and hungry, wanting a fire and a soft bed. He wondered how Lura was and envied her jail cell. At least it had a bed and wasn't cold. Already, he was beginning to chill. He looked up through the bare trees, with very little sunlight reaching the forest floor. His thoughts wandered to his parents, wondering who they were and if they were still alive. His dad had been an Upright and his mother an Infirm. He'd been taken at birth and raised in a dome in Georgia until he was sixteen. He had to pee, so he did.

~

Fifty-two's next game-day assignment was on the southside, where lived the mentally ill. It was a fifteen-minute walk to the three-story flats, all made of yellow brick. The flats were large and had a separate bathroom. There was an extra level of security to keep them in, and 52 scanned his ID at the main entrance. The five buildings were arranged in a pentagon fashion with a small park and benches in the middle. He scanned into building A and proceeded to the first door on the left. He met another Upright in the hall with her patient, headed to the park. He nodded. She nodded.

He knocked and held his badge to the scanner. The door clicked open. The room was filled with natural light from the large, uncovered window. Barb Wheeler was sitting in her recliner in front of the Chatty. She turned and looked at him as if he were an alien. She balled up and held her hands like claws to her chest.

"Just me," said 52. He approached with measured, small steps. "It's game day." He felt the bottom drop out of his existence.

Barb made weird chewing motions, her eyes wide with wonder or fear. "It's game day."

"Yeah, game day."

"Oh, it's game day.

"Game day."

"Game day."

Barb was in her forties, slack-jawed, and had a bun of red hair. Her expression was generally blank. She sat in her chair and stared at the Chatty for hours, sometimes soiling herself there.

"Did you eat your breakfast?" said 52.

"Did you eat your breakfast?" said Barb. She smacked her lips. "I'm hungry." She wore the green pants and shirts of the mentally Infirm. Drool stained her shirt.

Fifty-two checked the bin and found the Scrumptious and a pack of cigarettes, filtered Koalas. "You forgot to eat," said 52. Her med cocktail for schizophrenia was incorporated into the Scrumptious. He opened the bag, handed her the block, and pocketed the cigarettes.

Barb didn't break out the cubes and put them to her mouth, gnawing with her crooked teeth. She had a following in domes out west and was often taped and then watched by the Uprights there. She had no idea that she was prayed to as a saint.

"Good girl," said 52.

The Chatty played a nature channel, showing a badger digging a hole. He turned to the news channel, and there was the panel of experts discussing Lura's appearance before the judge. The session had been streamed live from the jail. Behind them, the video of her played, sitting at a table. The moderator was Jeffrey Jeffs, a local celebrity. He was tall and suffered from Klinefelter's as well as Turner's syndrome. His head was small, his face oddly shaped like a woman's. The topic was Lura's body language and what it meant.

"Her head was down," said one. He was a Cyclops. "She's being submissive. She knows what's coming."

"But what about her outburst at the end? She told him to go to hell," said Jeffs.

"She's riding shotgun with death," said another.

"Yes, the judge had the last word," said Jeffs. "How about that scowl, her plea of innocence."

Fifty-two shook his head. Lura was a dead duck, unless something grand happened. He found the Parcheesi board in a corner of the room and set it up on the wooden table. There was only one dice, but Barb wouldn't know the difference. He helped her to stand and walked her to the table, handing her the Scrumptious.

"So, how ya been?" said 52. "Seen any goblins lately?" He let the pawns filter through his hand.

"So, how ya been?" said Barb.

Fifty-two knew they were being filmed and kept a lid on it. "Yes, my words exactly."

Barb laughed a stony laugh, coming from her throat.

"Here, I'll roll for you." He tossed the die onto the board. "Five! Fantastic, five!" He moved a pawn onto the board. There were dead spaces on the board since only two were playing, but 52 fudged the game, keeping the pieces moving until she had won. "Fantastico! You're the big winner."

"You're the big winner," said Barb. Her eyes glazed, and she held up her hands as if warding off a demon, which she was. Her face twisted, and she gasped.

"Okay, now simmer down, sweetheart." He watched her mouth writhe, and her hands twist in the air.

"They love me," said Barb. "I am loved." She seemed to relax and slumped her shoulders, her face inches from the table.

"Oh, yeah, sweetheart, you are loved no doubt," said 52.

There was breaking news on the Chatty, an update on the Merry Woodsmen. They had escaped, leaving behind all of their belongings, but Squad was searching. The faces of Chad and Davies appeared, and the commentator had very nice things to say about them. They had actually spent the night in the woods and would remain there until they caught the villains. Fifty-two longed to be in the woods with Jack, away from the Infirm.

Fifty-two pretended to play another game with Barb and then walked her back to her recliner. He made a point of kissing the top of her head and patting her on the shoulder. On to the next one.

He took the stairs to two, passed another Upright, and decided he would try to get Alvin Keys outside into the park. There were gingko trees there and flowers, and he longed for a break. Inside, as expected, he found Alvin pacing across the room, counting his footsteps. There had to be twenty-three, and Alvin was counting loudly. After twenty-three steps, he snapped his fingers three times and turned around again.

"Alvin? You counting?"

Alvin stopped and looked his way as if he were a piece of furniture. He clapped his hands five times and touched his toes. "Yes."

"How about we go to the park and pitch pennies. You like that, right? You can count outside for a while. Be good for you."

"Going outside to count, five times." He clapped five times and touched his toes.

"Great," said 52. He saluted the Chatty, which was on the sex channel, a woman with an extra leg coming from her chest being pumped in the ass by an Upright. He was stroking the extra leg.

"Great, great, great," said Alvin. He touched his head five times, counting each one.

"Put on your slippers, big boy," said 52. He hunted, found the black slippers, and put them in front of Alvin's feet.

Alvin was flexible. He leaned over and put the shoes on and off three times. Fifty-two took ten old pennies from a little glass bowl on the table. It took a while to get Alvin outside. He had to touch each doorknob, say "doorknob," and cough with his fist to his mouth five times.

Outside, Alvin settled down somewhat, counting off twenty-three steps, stopping, and then starting again. There was a circular sidewalk, and 52 explained that they would pitch pennies from a distance of ten feet, landing them on the sidewalk.

Alvin looked up toward the distant dome and sneezed. He then had to fake sneeze four more times. He took a penny from 52 and hurled it as hard as he could, overshooting the sidewalk by twenty feet.

"Can't win that way," said 52. He sighed and pitched a penny, landing it on the sidewalk. "See, like that. Come on, Alvin, you can do it."

"Yes, I can do it!" said Alvin. He turned around five times and touched his toes. He pitched the penny high into the air, and it landed near his feet. He screeched and kissed his forearm five times.

"Oh, Lord," said 52. "One of those days." For another ten minutes, they pitched pennies, losing half of them in the grass. He convinced Alvin to sit on a bench, and 52 tried to relax, enjoying the scenery. An Upright passed, pushing a decrepit woman in a wheelchair. Five minutes passed, and Alvin demanded to go back to his room.

"Twenty-three!" said Alvin over and over. "Twenty-three!"

Fifty-two led Alvin back inside and suffered through the rituals as they walked. Finally, back in the flat, 52 left, Alvin pacing back and forth twenty-three steps, counting in his loud, stony voice.

~

Lura was livid and stood in the middle of her cell, recounting the session with the judge. "God, I need some Champy. Think Gomer has more?"

"Yeah," said Mae. She pouted out her big lips. "It'll cost you, though. He knows you're desperate."

"I guess I'd do just about anything. Looks like the next thing for me is sentencing. Not even a trial. Just the damn judge deciding my fate." Lura growled.

"Look, babydoll, you just need to simmer down. None of this fretting will help you. It's game day. How about a game of dominoes? Play on my bed. What about it?"

"Ugh, I hate game day. I've never liked games and hate playing them with the Infirm. But, hell, there's nothing else to do. I'll play." She slapped the wall.

"But we have to have stakes," said Mae. "What'll it be, sex? Champy?"

"Really?" said Lura. "No to sex. Champy, I suppose, although we don't have any."

"You'll just owe me, or I'll owe you. Makes it more interesting, right?"

"Yeah, the Infirm love to gamble. A lot of them fly out to Las Vegas and gamble there. Supposed to be like a regular circus. I never played games, even when I was little. I hated studying for the game tests.”

“Yep, I remember the tests and the punishments,” said Mae. “You ever had an idea who your parents might have been?”

“Not really. I grew up in the dome at Auburn. Supposedly, they were professors who had been modified from Upright to Infirm. My group was raised by a cranky old bitch named Elmira and an Upright, her lackey, a young guy by the name of Matthew. I guess they’re still alive. I’d like to see them again.”

Mae sighed. “I met my mother by accident; did I tell you that? She works in Central. Apparently, she’s rich. She sponsored a ‘fun day’ for ‘exemplary’ Uprights at the park. There was lemon soda and Scrumptious, which was sweet. We didn’t really do anything except walk around and talk.”

“How did you meet your mother?” said Lura.

“Well, she was there, at the picnic. She rigged the whole event, I think, just to have a chance to meet me. I was sitting on a bench, and she came over and sat beside me. For some reason, as soon as she did that, I knew who she was and broke down crying. That drew attention, of course, and she just whispered ‘I love you’ and then left. That was over a year ago. Haven’t seen her since.”

“Huh,” said Lura. “My guess is my parents are in Auburn. Not sure. I liked it there, had my friends, and then got shipped here. That was over ten years ago.”

"Yep, everybody has a mom somewhere," said Mae. She squatted on the toilet and took a pee.

Just then, Gomer passed by, staring at Mae.

"Fuck off," said Mae.

"Hey, Gomer," said Lura. "What about some more Champy. We're out."

Gomer licked his dry lips and patted his potbelly. "Fresh out myself. What's the trade gonna be? I'll make it a priority if the price is right." He laughed in a little burst, kind of a giggle. "I'll even arrange to work nights. Not so many noses sniffing around."

"What are you proposing?" said Mae.

"Anal sex," said Gomer. "In the sweet ass. Just one of you, but I'll give you each two doses." He giggled again.

Lura didn't bat an eye. "Three doses each, and I'll sacrifice my ass. You're disgusting, by the way."

"Lura?" said Mae. "He could have the clap."

"Yeah, with a condom, though." Lura scowled at Gomer.

"Easy now, but it's a deal. I'll wrangle a shift for tomorrow night. It'll be sex day anyway, right?"

"Lura, you'll regret it," said Mae.

"Well, that's a given," said Lura.

"Shake on it?" said Gomer. He put his hand through the bars.

Lura looked at the flaccid hand. She took it and pumped once. "Deal, asshole."

Gomer whistled. "Such language, but it's a deal." He grinned and walked away, headed down the long hall.

"You crazy, babydoll?" said Mae.

"Yeah, but I have a plan. We'll get the Champy beforehand. I think we can both take him, take his stun gun, and blast him. We'll hide the Champy. He won't be able to do anything about it."

"Whoa," said Mae. "Do you want solitary?"

"Well, maybe I do." Lura leaned against the wall. "Heck, maybe we could escape. We can steal his keys to open the doors. If I can make it outside, I'll head for the sewers. Worth a try, right? They're gonna hang me anyway, right?"

"Well, maybe so, but I'm not eager to swing with you. You'll have to escape by yourself. I'll be out of here within six months, I hope."

"Yeah, I get it," said Lura. "God, I feel like a hardened criminal already. Have I said that already? Strange what this place can do to you. But I don't think I can bear to see that judge's face again. I'd like to think that Jack has some plan to rescue me, but that seems like a long shot, especially if they catch him."

"Damn, girl. I admire your spunk. I'll just be the innocent bystander, say that Gomer tried to attack you. I can do that much."

Lura grinned, her eyes afraid.

~

With late afternoon approaching, Chad and Davies stopped to rest, letting their heavy packs slide to the ground. The helicopter had gotten close enough to use the two-way radio, but there had been no useful news, and they had just continued more or less north, coming across old foundations and a few old roads. Chad did more pushups, while Davies took a long drink of water and ate a bite of Scrumptious.

"When the hell do we stop?" said Davies. He rubbed his big ear, making it red.

"I guess nightfall. There must be something they're headed to, a destination, maybe a cabin or an old house. The terrain is supposed to get pretty rugged soon. Maybe another cave."

"Like looking for a needle in a haystack if you ask me," said Davies.

"I bet they'll build a fire. Maybe we should keep looking until it gets really dark. Fire will give them away." Chad popped his knuckles and scratched his leg.

"Well, that's a thought, but this pack is damn heavy."

"We could stash the packs and do a big circle once the sun goes down," said Chad.

"Huh," said Davies. "You're serious about catching these guys."

"Yeah, we'll be heroes. We've already made the news. Maybe we'll get privileges, extra Champy, cigarettes, alcohol. Could be worth it."

"If you say so," said Davies. "I figured I'd outlast you, old man."

"Hey, I'm only forty-two." Chad puffed out his chest and yelled. "See?"

"Ha, I guess you'll take them down single-handedly. I'll be your backup. They do have that rifle, though. Don't want to get shot."

"Yeah, but we've got these." Chad patted the Lockmeyer on his belt. "If we somehow lose each other, just fire into the air."

"Should we separate, do it that way?"

"I don't think so. We need to stick together. There's three of them," said Chad. "Okay, let's move."

They hoisted their packs. Within an hour, they reached the first small but steep canyon, having to climb down backwards, holding onto saplings and rocks. At the bottom was a frigid stream, and then it was a steep climb. They took it at a 45-degree angle, huffing their way to the top and more rolling terrain. Another two hours passed, and they had negotiated the smaller canyons, soon coming to an old two-lane road. Chad stumbled across a guardrail covered with kudzu and fell on his face. Davies laughed, while Chad cursed.

"That funny, huh?" said Chad. He brushed himself off and adjusted his pack. "Maybe here is where we leave the packs and do a big circle. Looks like we have another hour of light." The sun was setting in the west.

"Good by me," said Davies. "Which way, commander? Left or right?"

"I say right. Maybe we do a five-mile loop or close to it. Take us a couple of hours. When we hit this road again, it'll lead us back here. Keep our eyes peeled."

"Alrighty then," said Davies, and they were off, their backpacks hidden in the kudzu.

~

The sun had disappeared, leaving the canyon in a deep funk of shadows and weird light. The only sound was that of the waterfall, sounding expensive, like a natural wonder that deserved a hefty fee to enjoy. Ismael had surprised them with a can that he'd found in the basement along the way. Opened with his pocketknife, all three peered into the liquid that looked dark brown. It was a can of beef stew with potatoes, and they each got a solid mouthful, groaning with pleasure at the tastes and the rush of normalcy into their bones.

The room behind the waterfall led back about thirty feet and rose twenty feet. A flat, gravelly area made a great sleeping spot. Ismael was the fire starter as usual, and soon he had a large one blazing, crackling, and popping.

"Wish we had that damn radio," said Bard. They had arranged three big rocks around the fire. The smoke went straight up and slid out beneath the waterfall.

"Wish with one hand and spit in the other," said Ismael.

Jack puzzled that one, holding his cold hands to the flames, dreading the long, cold night.

"So, tell us again about that damn judge," said Bard. "I remember him. Nasty old man. Had his kidneys removed and replaced with ones from a pig. Had one crazy eye that looked around like it was alive. Like it might have arms and legs."

"That's him," said Jack. "Well, I never liked him, especially on sex day. Treated me like a damn dog."

"He told you to lick his balls," said Ismael. He put another large chunk of wood on the fire.

"Yep," said Jack. "And it was damn foot-care day. He didn't care what day it was, but I did. Had me some big wire cutters for those big nasty toenails."

"Oh, baby," said Bard. "Wire cutters. Hot dog."

"Well, I told him no, and that set him off. Finally, I said, "Sure," and then I went in with those wire cutters like I was crazy. Something just came over me. He was pounding on me, but I kept at it. Got most of it."

Ismael shuddered, his feet to the fire. "And then you stuffed the mess into his mouth?"

"Indeed, I did," said Jack. "But then I panicked and ran. I ducked into the nearest building and tried a couple of doors, but no one would let me in. Then Lura's door opened."

"Damn boy, you must have been high on adrenaline. Did you plan to do it?"

"Well," said Jack. "I'd thought about strangling him. On sex day, he liked for me to choke him a bit. I just snapped."

"Temporary insanity, I'd say." Bard clapped his hands, the sound echoing in the sloping chamber.

"If they could prove you were insane, then you could become one of the elite," said Ismael. "Maybe that's your angle, if you get caught. Just keep acting crazy."

"Hmm, hadn't thought about that," said Jack.

"Yeah, we'll vouch for you if we get caught," said Bard. "Tell 'em how you acted strange and heard voices."

"Anyway, I popped into Lura's room, and she was high on Champy. It just hit me that I could be pretending to carry her to the hospital for cover, and that's what I did. Squad got after us and couldn't get her into the sewer. Had to leave her, dammit. Shit, I think about that all day."

"The plan is to spring her, right? Start a goddamn uprising." Bard stomped his boot on the gravel.

"I wish," said Jack. "God, I'm such a loser, getting her mixed up in this." He pulled back from the hot flames burning his face and put his feet forward.

"Don't fret, you'll be the hero in the end. I can almost smell it," said Bard.

"It won't be easy," said Ismael. "Have to be realistic, right?"

"Come on, Frowny Fred," said Bard. "We have to dream big. Things could be changing. The Uprights won't stand for a hanging, especially of a pretty woman. We can count on it."

"I'm just saying," said Ismael. He poked the fire, rearranging the burning limbs. The end of a ten-foot log lay in the fire, and he advanced it a foot or so, sending up sparks.

"Hey, we found each other, and that's a near miracle," said Bard. "I got a good feeling. Hell, we're the Merry Woodsmen, we got that, but all we do is run and interfere here and there. We need greatness, right?"

Ismael cleared his throat. "First, we need freedom. That's more or less what we agreed to, right? To just be free."

Bard thought. "Well, we're free, right?"

"But for how long?" said Ismael.

"Look, this had better work, because I don't want your blood on my hands any more than Lura's," said Jack. "I trust you guys, though. I'm willing to do just about anything."

"No telling what's coming, but it's bound to be good," said Bard. He grinned, showing his big teeth. With his wild brown hair, he looked a bit crazy.

Jack said, "Thanks," and sank into a mild funk, worried about the collision of events to come.

Chad and Davies sweated as they walked, even though the darkness had plunged the forest into a cold funk. They crossed several small streams and deduced there must be a large creek or river nearby. They walked single file, small branches cracking beneath their feet, rocks catching the tips of their boots. The moon was not out, but the sky was choked with stars that cast dim shadows on the damp forest floor.

"Are we heading northwest still?" said Davies.

Chad stared at the compass in the dim light. "Yeah, more or less. Let's hope we don't have to cross anything deep. I'd hate to drown at night."

"Well, that's comforting," said Davies.

They trudged on and indeed came to a small river, it seemed. They could hear the water rushing over rocks and against the bank.

"Damn, let's go north another mile or so and then keep circling back." Chad stood with his hands on his hips. He picked up a rock and threw it into the water with a *bloop.*

Davies picked up a large stick and threw it upstream. The stick came rushing back at them. "Maybe you're right."

Chad glanced at his compass and headed north, weaving between large trees and brush. His leg tangled in a briar wad and ripped his pants. "Well, damn." He extricated himself, and they wound forward, passing through large limestone boulders and then into somewhat clear forest, the ground soft with leaves and pine straw.

On they walked for twenty minutes, and Chad determined that they should head west for a while. The terrain was rough and hilly, but seemed to be going uphill. For another half hour, they walked and heard the sound of a waterfall.

"Waterfall?" said Davies.

"Yeah, let's drink."

They moved forward, and a chasm appeared to open ahead of them. In the starlight, they could see the top of the waterfall as it sluiced over an edge of rocks.

"You smell smoke?" said Chad. He held up his hand.

Davies crept toward the edge of the abyss, which loomed like a dark hole. He could see into the tops of giant trees growing from the bottom. "What's that?"

Chad came up behind him. "It has to be a fire. Son, we have found our quarry." His breath caught.

They whispered.

"But how the hell do we get down there? Wait till daylight?" said Davies.

"No, this time we'll surprise them. There has to be a way down. Come on."

Davies followed Chad, headed away from the

waterfall. Ten minutes and still no way down.

"Let's just wait till daylight. No use breaking our necks."

"Hell no. Keep walking," and soon they came to a crack in the rock ledge that seemed to be a natural staircase down. "I'll go first," said Chad.

Chad braced himself into the crack and descended. He couldn't see bottom. He slipped, gasped, and caught a sapling growing in the crack. "Damn." He reached his foot down, but there was only air. Defeated, he clambered back to the top. "We'll just have to keep going this way."

Davies said, "Are you sure?"

"I'm sure," said Chad.

Glowing coals of orange simmered within the fire. The three sat there staring into the flames, as if it were telling them a story. All were tired but drawn by the heat.

"I miss my bed," said Jack. "Sad to say it."

"Hell, I don't," said Bard. "The ground's better than any bed, especially when you're free."

"Why haven't you guys ventured farther? Why do you stay in the area?" said Jack.

"It's the land," said Ismael. "I feel connected to it, like it's my natural home. Go too far, and things will change. Out west, there's deserts. I can't imagine living in a desert."

"Yep, he said it. Something in my bones says this is home, and we need to share it with more folks like us. If enough of us get out of here, maybe they'd leave us alone. Cut their losses."

"Could be a pipe dream," said Ismael. "What about you? How does all of this make you feel? You want to go back just for a bed?"

"Well, I do like it. It's beautiful out here. But there's no food, except at that wama, and that would run out quick with more people." Jack stood and stretched, his eyes aching from gazing into the fire.

In a flash, Ismael was up. A shot rang out, and he grabbed the rifle and pointed it into the darkness beyond the fire.

"Put the gun down, boy! We've got you covered!" said Chad. "Stun grenades here if you need one to crack your bones!" He fired a shot into the fire for effect, hot coals jumping.

"The fuck," said Bard. "Get up here where we can see you and fight fair!"

"I don't think so!" said Chad. "Put the gun down! Now! Or I'll shoot."

Ismael glanced at Bard, still sitting. Jack was standing. He put the rifle on the gravel.

"Okay, hands up, criminals," said Chad. He emerged into the light holding his pistol with one hand. Behind him, Davies appeared, visibly shaking, his pistol wavering toward them. "Hands up and sit. Do it."

Jack and Ismael sat, facing the fire.

"Turn towards us and keep your hands up," said Chad. He approached the side of the waterfall, mist hitting his uniform. The trio did as they were told.

Chad eased into the lit chamber, his gun aimed at Bard. Davies came in farther to his left.

"Remember me?" said Chad.

"Yeah, you're Chad," said Bard. "And I'd like to kick your ass."

"Ha," said Davies. He couldn't decide on a target and kept his gun traveling from one to the other.

"Well, good news and bad news," said Chad. He laughed.

"What's the bad news?" said Ismael.

"Well, it's obvious," said Chad. "We caught you with your pants down. Again. You should've known better than to build a fire."

Bard laughed. "Well, I sure would like to hear the good news."

Chad smiled. "We're here to join you." He glanced at Davies.

"What?" said Bard.

"What?" said Davies.

"Young Davies here is hearing this for the first time, but he's got no choice. We're joining you. I've always admired your brass balls, the Merry Woodsmen for god's sake." He lowered his pistol and holstered it. "Put your gun away, Davies."

Davies frowned, his heart beating in his throat. "What the hell? You can't do that. We'll get death."

"Better than that damn dome, now put your gun away!"

Davies did as he was told, stupefied.

~

The first thing they did the next morning was to hike back to the packs and eat. Everyone stuffed themselves with Scrumptious and then took long drinks of water. The plan was to lure the helicopter in, Davies and Chad saying they had captured the trio. For now, Davies and Chad would pretend to be hot on the trail of the three desperados while scheming to spring Lura from jail and the dome. With everyone on board, even the somewhat skittish Davies, they could move freely, and their first goal was to regain the radio back at the cave. They couldn't be seen walking together, so Davies and Chad left first, and then an hour later, Ismael, Jack, and Bard.

By four p.m., everyone was accounted for, and they sat outside in the late afternoon sun filtering down through the quiet trees. They'd had brief contact with the helicopter, Chad fudging his report to the pilot. He requested extra food rations to be dropped the next day. The pilot was under the impression that Davies and Chad would be scoping out the cave, confident that the trio would return for the radio. It would be the perfect trap, Chad had said.

Settled in and with an early fire burning outside the cave, they discussed possible plans for rescuing Lura.

"I think you're right," said Chad. "We want to wait until the death sentence has been made public. That will get everyone restless. Then, with a successful rescue and some propaganda, we just might be able to tip the cookie jar." He'd read about cookie jars.

"You think the pilot will really cooperate?" said Bard. "He might just fly us into the ground."

"No way," said Chad. "He's more likely than not to join us. It's the other Squad riding shotgun,

I'm worried about. We'll have to ditch them." Chad walked about, his uniform with little holes and tears from the briars. He looked fresh and alive, as if his life were finally coming together.

"What if Squad resists?" said Ismael. "Do we shoot them?"

"I'd hate to do that," said Davies. He was sitting cross-legged on the ground.

"Well," said Jack. "I say shoot if it's them or us."

"They're just a bunch of wet noses. They'll give in without a fight, I'm sure of it," said Bard.

"They're my friends," said Davies. He looked like a little revolutionary with his big ears and three-day beard. "I say we avoid killing anybody at all costs."

"Just tools," said Jack. "Give me a gun, and I'll shoot 'em in the legs."

"Well, we have the stun grenades," said Bard. "Could be useful."

They talked further, making a primary and a contingency plan. Once in the helicopter, they would land inside the dome. They would still need heads and hands on the inside to pull it off. The conversation turned.

"Hey, Jack, it's Sunday, sex day. Reckon the judge will want his rubber balls licked?" Bard laughed.

"Hell, I feel sorry for whoever has to deal with him," said Jack. "How long before he hands down Lura's sentence?"

"Could've happened today for all we know. Helicopter should be flying over sometime soon. We'll get an update," said Chad. "Hell, she could be executed the same day, especially if they figure in the possibility of retaliation. We'll have to move fast."

And just like that, the sounds of the helicopter in the distance, scrubbing the air like an old washboard. "Shit," said Bard. He, Ismael, and Jack slipped inside the cave. Chad got on the two-way. "Over, one-nine, over."

The helicopter was perhaps a mile away and closing. "Copy, Squad, over."

Chad updated the pilot on their waiting game and asked about any news from the dome on Lura.

"Nothing new today, over. Sex day, so no doubt the judge is preoccupied. Come Monday, he should be shaking the trees, over." The pilot began to circle and spotted them on the ground. "Nice fire. You guys need anything?"

"Yeah," said Chad. "Food. We're famished, burning calories like crazy. Drop a week's supply tomorrow, if you don't mind, and maybe a couple of blankets. Gets cold out here, but you wouldn't know, over."

"Yeah, better you than me," said the pilot. He laughed. His protruding front teeth brushed the microphone. "Okay, one more grid for me today. Guys in the back are starting to whine, over and out."

"Out," said Chad. He waved. The Squad, peering out the open cargo door, waved.

"Well, that was easy," said Davies. He threw a small rock into the fire.

"Easy for now," said Chad. He dropped and did fifty push-ups, waiting for the helicopter's droning to disappear.

Ismael peeked out to make sure no one new had joined them on the ground. He motioned for the others, and they crawled out.

"Any news?" said Bard.

"Nothing new today. Tomorrow could get hot, though. Have to be ready," said Chad. "If worse comes to worst, maybe they'll give us the option to become Infirm, chop our legs off, and remove a kidney." He laughed.

"I'd rather die," said Ismael.

"Me too," said Jack.

~

The judge slept late, his first night back in his flat. His groin ached from the extensive surgery, and he figured it would be anal today. He sat in his bed, leaning against two pillows, watching the Chatty, the sex channel, to get himself warmed up. He checked the clock on the wall, ten, and wondered where his Upright was. He'd requested a woman this time and bumped his lobster claws together. On the Chatty, a large black man was rimming a sixteen-year-old girl. His tongue was extra-long. The judge licked his lips, thinking about his aching taint.

There was a knock at the door, and the judge released it with the button on the back of his tooth. The young woman who appeared was Cassidy. He eyed her as she hesitated and walked in sideways.

"Well, good morning, sunshine," said the judge. "You can call me Chet. Fetch my Scrumptious, and then we can get it on."

"Yessir," said Cassidy. She had light blonde hair in a bun, with wisps lingering over her neck as if filled with static electricity. She held a small bag. She went to the bin and retrieved the medicated Scrumptious, impregnated with the judge's meds. Like a trapped animal, she seemed to move backward with every move of his forward. "Here."

"Glass of water, sweetheart." He popped a cube in his mouth and chewed. "So, Cassidy, you're a lucky girl. Not just anyone gets to rub shoulders with the judge." He took the glass of water in his lobster hand and spilled a little. "Rats." He sipped and chewed, his eyes glued to Cassidy. "Might as well get them clothes off. Got something special I want to show you."

Cassidy shuddered, hearing her name come from his mouth. She watched his lazy eye roam around the room. "Uh, let's eat first." She folded her arms across her chest.

"Are you questioning me?" He chewed slower.

"Uh, no, sir." She kept her back turned to the Chatty. "Mind if I get a glass of water?"

"Well, sweetheart, help yourself. My water is your water. I hear you come from Laramore. You weren't a bad girl, were you? You know they only send me the best. That damn Jack had been with me for over a year. I had him pegged as harmless, but I was wrong."

"How about the news? Want to watch the news?"

"Why in hell would I want to watch the news? I am the news." He chewed another cube. "But change it if you like. Or I will." The channel changed. A panel of experts was discussing Squad's strategy to set a trap in the cave for the Merry

Woodsmen. They were all dressed in formal attire, sitting around a hexagonal table.

"So, what do you know about this Jack? We'll catch him soon and then..." The judge drew the thumb of his lobster claw across his throat and took a big drink. "Put this on the table, would you, sweetheart?"

Cassidy took the glass and the uneaten Scrumptious. His hand brushed hers, and she flinched.

"Gassed up and ready to go, sweetheart. Come a little closer, so daddy can show you his specials." He pushed down his pants with the cut-off legs and spread his knees apart. "Just look. Titanium inside latex with some soft balls in there."

Cassidy took a step backward, a look of horror on her face. The judge's groin had been sewn together, the prosthetic looking like the real thing except permanently erect.

"Come here and touch it. I can't feel anything, but I want to see your hand down there. Be gentle now."

Cassidy froze.

The judge frowned. "Do it, sweetheart!" His voice deepened. He laughed.

Cassidy took three steps forward, leaned in, and touched it. It felt like rubber. She stepped back.

"What's the matter, sweetheart, cat got your tongue?"

"No, sir. It's just...that you need to rest. You could tear something, and have to go to the hospital."

"Well, now, that's why you have to be gentle with good old Chet. Can you say my name, Chet? Not many get the privilege."

"Chet," said Cassidy, the word seeming to burn her lips.

"Okay, now we're gonna stick with anal today, okay? You bring the strap-on like you were told?"

"Yessir."

"Well, first, you get naked. Now."

Cassidy looked around the room, knowing that she was being filmed, that she would most likely end up on the sex channel. She slipped off her shoes and pulled down her pants, revealing tan panties. She pulled off her shirt.

"Mmm," said the judge. "All the way, my little bitch." His lazy eye jerked. He gazed at her small, perky breasts, her large nipples.

Cassidy slid down her panties. Thick pubic hair covered her mound of Venus, just the way the judge liked it. He was old-fashioned. She folded her arms and crossed her legs as if a magic wind would whisk her away.

"Chet wants you to wear that strap-on, real bad." His respirations became deeper and quicker.

"Yes, Chet." She stepped into the leg loops and tightened the straps of the erect silicone penis. It even matched her skin tone, just a shade off white.

"I'm gonna roll over real careful. You might even help Chet. He doesn't want to fall off the bed. And don't forget the lube."

Cassidy grimaced and helped him turn over. His butt was fat and jiggly, pasty white. She reached into the bag for the lubricant and squirted some on the end of the dildo.

"Gentle now with Chet. He's sore down there."

Cassidy swallowed and put a knee on the bed. She spread his amputated legs and saw the hairy hole surrounded by skin tags and heaved. She tried to recall a nature show, one about a little raccoon named Teddy. She disembodied herself and soon heard the judge groaning, half in pain, half in pleasure.

~

Monday, foot care day, and Jack awoke, wrapped in a piece of plastic, sweating. The small fire and the body heat of the other four seemed to warm the cave. As usual, Ismael was up and about. Bard was drinking a cup of water warmed on the fire, and Chad and Davies were still asleep inside their sleeping bags. Jack was getting used to sleeping on the ground and wondered what the next few days would hold.

"Those sleepy heads need to wake up. Need some of that scrumptious Scrumptious. Not that I've missed it all these months," said Bard. He clapped his hands and got the two Squad squirming.

"Just get it out of my bag," said Chad. He yawned. "Should be dropping more today."

Davies stirred. "Got a crick in my neck." He sat up, rubbing it.

"You guys have any coffee?" said Ismael.

"No, just the tea," said Chad. "In the bag."

"Tea works," said Ismael. "Everyone want tea?"

Murmurs of yes made the rounds.

"Should hear something about Lura today," said Chad. "The judge is gonna want to get her ass in the frying pan as soon as possible." He did twenty standing squats.

"At least she won't have to cut toenails again," said Bard. "Almost as bad as sex day."

"God, be gentle. She's my girl," said Jack. "But being hunted is worth missing foot care day. I'll never be able to go back to that life, not that I would be allowed, cutting off the judge's balls."

"Yeah, that should serve as a warning to the rest of those fucked up fuckers," said Chad. "Better than any protest or petition."

"Do you think we could get our jobs back?" said Davies. He was the youngest of the group and the most attached to the dome.

"Hell, no," said Chad. "We crossed the line. I know you were caught by surprise with this, but you have to admit there is a higher cause here. Even Squad are basically slaves."

"Yeah, that was a real shocker. I wish you had warned me. I might have backed out...not that I'm afraid." Davies crawled from his bag, rolled to his knees, and stood.

"We're in this together now," said Chad. "Any reservations, the time has passed. You know too much, and we need you for the rescue." He was as excited about the possibility of creating a riot as Bard and Ismael. Jack just wanted to set Lura free.

The five sat around the fire, chewing their breakfast and drinking hot tea. They worked out the details of how they would acquire the helicopter and force the pilot to fly it to the dome. There was a retractable pane that the helicopter would pass through before landing. But first, they needed Lura to be sentenced to death, for the Uprights to get crazy and create a distraction. The faithful on the inside were to spread rumors of an uprising to maximize participation.

"Radio contact in fifteen minutes," said Bard. "Let's get it outside."

He and Ismael set up the antenna, stringing it between two trees. Ismael tuned to 612.550, hearing only static and bloopy noises. Another ten minutes passed, and the static went blank.

"Fire and ladder, pronto. Fire and ladder, pronto."

"Pronto, lemon squeezebox. Pronto, lemon squeezebox."

The others were coming out of the cave to listen.

"What's the news, good buddy? Over," said Bard.

"All quiet for now, but rumors spreading. All on alert to hear word of the fate of Lura, over."

"Time frame for a sentence, over?" said Bard.

"Expected today. Let's talk again at seventeen hundred. Will need to move quickly, over."

"We have a plan," said Bard. "Can't release the details. Too risky. But we have access to the dome via the copter when the time comes, over." He withheld the desertion of Davies and Chad. That would just have to be a surprise.

"Really? Is the plan to take her out through the sewer? Over."

"Let's call that plan B. If we fail to access the dome, then she will need to be led there. We'll meet her on the other side. Someone will be in the tunnel to greet her at the right place, over."

"Got it. Will diffuse the information through the usual channels. No sign of a breach as of yet. Us Uprights are naturally tight-lipped. Thirty seconds, over."

"Well, that's about it, over," said Bard. "Hopefully see you soon, perhaps two days if all goes according to plan, over."

"Sounds..." and the static returned.

Bard shut down the radio with the flick of a switch. "Something's up. He just cut off." He frowned.

Ismael shook his head. "Damn, maybe they nailed him. They'll have our channel. We can't use it again, unless we have to."

"Well, that's fucked," said Chad. "You'll just have to guess now."

"We're still going in, though, right?" said Jack. "I'll sneak in by myself if necessary."

Bard waved him off. "The Merry Woodsmen now number five. We're in this together. Maybe at the end of this, we'll be a hundred, a thousand, ladies included."

"I'm all for it, but Lura is what's important here," said Jack.

"She's key, but there's the larger picture," said Chad. "I didn't desert for just one woman. My life is at stake here, and so is yours."

"Well, did we invite you?" said Jack, clenching his fists.

"Like it or not, I'd say you did, especially these two." Chad nodded at Bard and Ismael. "I'm here for freedom, not this Lura, even though she will be a trigger. She may have to be sacrificed."

"Look, asshole, you can get your Squad tails back to the dome. Lura is the object here, and if she helps the larger cause, then fine." Jack stared at Chad, who just dropped and did twenty pushups.

"Okay, gentlemen," said Bard. "We have to work together. You're both right. No one knows how this will work out. Jack, it could happen that Lura is left behind. There's no guarantee of anything. Most Squad are loyal to the Infirm."

Jack fumed. "I'll make sure she gets out, regardless. We're risking our lives by just being here. We have nothing to lose. Infirm be damned. Davies? Are you with us? You're awfully quiet."

"Uh, yeah, except the part about giving my life."

"But your life is damned, boy," said Bard. "You are part of this, unless you turn and run. Of course, we'd have to shoot you. Don't forget that. You could ruin the whole thing."

"Can we trust him?" said Ismael. He was sitting cross-legged on the pine straw.

"Of course we can," said Chad. "Right, Davies?"

"Right," said Davies. He turned and walked away.

~

Cornelius Fava was worried. Several Upright had not reported to work on time. He wore his video helmet, his head jerked to the right, and he reclined in his wheelchair, speaking with members of the Council.

"My Upright says there's rumors of an uprising,"

said Leroy. He only used the audio portion of his helmet, his missing eyes leaking gooey fluid.

"You've said that, but we've heard it before," said Fava. "And what's the word from Squad. Have they located the delinquent Uprights who missed their appointments this morning?"

Daria Levitts, Squad liaison, spoke. "A half dozen were found in the flat of an Upright, Tyson. Something's definitely up. They were reprimanded and sent to their clients. We're holding and questioning Tyson." Daria's arms were sewn together behind her back, giving her a pigeon chest. She had been reprogrammed from Upright to Infirm as a reward for forty years of faithful service.

"Troubling," said Cornelius.

Peter Peters, the dwarf with brittle bone disease, spoke. "I'd say Squad should be put on full alert, especially with the sentencing of Lura approaching. My Upright has said there are rumors she will be put to death, which is most likely the case. Could be a tricky situation. Any links between that and the gathering this morning?"

Cornelius cleared his throat. "Mrs. Butts, would you address that?"

Butts was sweating like a stuck hog as usual. The inside of her video helmet screen was smeared. "We'll know more after we question this Tyson character. There was definitely a meeting of some sort. Could be linked, but we're not sure."

"Well," said Cornelius. "Let's make sure that we are sure. I want everyone here to be extra attentive. Daria, I want you to meet with Colonel Faccia and have him update you. I'd hate to have any Squad involved in this chicanery."

"Yes, sir," said Daria. "Will do." Her tailbone itched, and she scratched it. Her knees had been removed, but she was preparing to have her legs cut off as they were in the way now. The gene therapy for sickle cell anemia was going well. Already, she'd had one vicious attack that had required IV pain meds.

"Well, another day in the dome," said Cornelius. "Let's meet again at noon and reassess, shall we?" He looked at his comrades gathered on the screen, wondering perhaps if there was a traitor among them.

~

Inside 5400, Gretchen told Darla Doppel goodbye and headed with her footcare kit to the next flat, Gregory Nixon. She knocked, scanned, and entered. The room smelled like the inside of a shoe. Gregory had transferred himself to his motorized chair and was eating Scrumptious in front of the Chatty. He was very tall, too tall, and had bone spreaders screwed into his legs to make him taller. He had trouble sitting up, from keeping his head from flopping onto his lap. Diabetes and high blood pressure rounded out his portfolio. He'd had one stroke as a result, and his left side was very weak.

"Hey," said Gretchen. "Tidy up your toes?" She glanced at the Chatty. It was breaking news. The Squad on patrol for the outlaw trio had spent the night in the forest again. They would most likely be awarded the Bright Star and given a parade, regardless of what happened. The forest was full of bears, wolves, stinging bees, and even deer that could gore you with their antlers.

Gregory had a headache. "Can you send for some aspirin? I don't feel well."

"Sure," said Gretchen. She hit the red button above the bin and ordered the aspirin. She'd had her Champy the night before and felt like a million bucks.

"Okay, gotta get on your feet. Got a line a mile long waiting." She squatted in front of Gregory and removed his soft blue house shoes. The nail on his right big toe was ingrown, making the surrounding flesh proud and angry. "Oh, gotta fix that one. Hurt?" She pinched the toe.

"Goddamn! Girl, be careful."

Gretchen tried not to grin. "Gonna make a V in the end of the nail to relieve pressure on the sides." That was standard for ingrown nails. She took her big clippers and cut the first line of the V. The nail was thick and popped, releasing a little cloud of powdery smoke. She cut the second line, and a chunk of nail flew between her legs. "Got it." She then trimmed the nail and moved down the line of toes, soon reaching the other foot. The nail on his little toe seemed to be loose, and she pinched it with heavy-duty tweezers. She twisted the nail, and it slid out, a fat drop of blood forming on the nailbed. "Well, shit." She took a bit of gauze and dabbed at the blood. Since he was diabetic, she checked his pedal pulses and examined the skin for breaks. His feet were covered with tiny blue veins that looked painful.

"Thanks," said Gregory. He was more or less glued to the breaking news, which was really just an update. As soon as the panel of experts appeared, he turned his attention to his feet and to Gretchen squatting there. "I can see the part in your hair."

"Well, good for you," said Gretchen. "Very observant."

"No need to be a smartass," said Gregory.

"Or you'll report me, right? Okay, time to wash those toots." She fetched the washpan, squirted in some liquid soap, and ran hot water. Squatting, she put his foot in the water, and he jerked it back.

"No need to scald me, you little bitch."

"Hey, simmer down. You want cold water instead?"

"No. Just be careful. I have diabetes, you know."

"Yeah, I know. That's why I'm doing a good job with your feet. Do they hurt?"

"Yeah, like a motherfucker, especially at night. Get all tingly."

"Okay, let's try this again." She lowered his foot into the pan and carefully scrubbed, and then the other foot. The water had turned a milky white. She took a small, dry towel and dried his feet, then slipped on his house shoes. "There, all done. Good to go." She'd been listening to the Chatty for clues about what might happen. There had been a meeting of Central that morning after reports of a sick-out. A Tyson had been detained, but she was sure she didn't know him. Maybe yesterday, that's what the woman had been talking about, the one who had approached her in the street, telling her that something big was in the works. "Need anything?"

"The aspirin?" said Gregory.

"Right." She retrieved the plastic baggie from the bin and brought it and a glass of water. He swallowed the pills. She said goodbye and left, headed across the hall to number three, a Suzy Quonset. She was a real doozy and liked her nails painted jet black.

Inside, Suzy was still in bed. She had one good leg, but the other was disabled, having had the femoral nerve severed. The foot had been bound with blocks to disfigure it.

"Still in bed? You okay?" said Gretchen. Suzy's wheelchair was beside her bed, and she had pretty good arm strength.

"Just waiting on you, pretty girl."

Gretchen smiled. "Mind if I do your feet in bed. Saves my back."

"Sure thing," said Suzy. She wiggled her big toe.

Gretchen placed her bag on the bed and pulled off the cream-colored sock. The foot looked swollen and was a pasty white. The nail polish from the week prior had begun to flake, and that was her first chore, to strip them. She took a small bottle of acetone and worked the black polish free, the foot jerking as if it was ticklish.

"Hurts," said Suzy, "like a shooting pain."

"Well, I'll be gentle," said Gretchen. She took her smaller clippers and trimmed the nails, then used an emery board to smooth them. She fixed a pan of soapy, hot water and went to work, washing the dead skin from between her toes. She dried the foot and then the other one. "Well, I guess I'm done here. Want your Scrumptious?"

"No, not feeling so well this morning."

The Chatty broadcast the chatter of the expert panel, some theorizing that trouble was afoot in the dome. That had brought a laugh since it was foot-care day.

Gretchen looked Suzy in the eyes and saw that something was amiss. She was pale and her breathing shallow. All of a sudden, she vomited and then stopped breathing, her eyes rolling back in her head. Gretchen ran to the wall and hit the emergency button.

"Emergency, what is the problem?" The Chatty screen had changed from the expert panel to the face of a wrinkled woman wearing a headset.

"Not breathing. Send help right away!" said Gretchen.

"Sending help," said the woman. "Fifty-four hundred, room three. Estimated time of arrival, eight minutes. Initiate CPR at five minutes, please."

Gretchen looked at Suzy, her mouth leaking vomit. She couldn't bring herself to do mouth-to-mouth and stood there helpless as the minutes ticked by.

"Five minutes passed. Initiate CPR!" said the woman. She could see Gretchen standing, doing nothing.

Gretchen stood over Suzy and began chest compressions. When she moved in to do the respirations, she faked it and returned to chest compressions. It seemed an eternity before help arrived, but two paramedics burst through the door and pushed her aside. Suzy was dead as a doornail, but they initiated an all-out assault to revive her, pumping her full of epinephrine, shocking her, and jamming a tube through her trachea into her lungs. They worked for ten long minutes without result and finally stopped. This would look bad on their record.

"Patient is deceased," said the larger of the two, both wearing bright blue jumpsuits. "We'll need a full accounting, ma'am."

The room was a wreck, as if it had been rifled, syringes on the floor, packaging strewn about, the bed askew. The woman on the Chatty disappeared, and the expert panel returned.

"She just stopped breathing," said Gretchen. "I have to get to my next patient." She toyed with her ponytail.

"Not so fast, ma'am. We need a full report. This is a serious matter." He then retrieved a computer tablet and began grilling her. It took about ten minutes, and a member of Squad appeared in the doorway with handcuffs.

"What in tarnation?" said Gretchen.

"Orders, ma'am," said the Squad. "We're on high alert. Haven't you been paying attention? This is the second death today, and then there was that sick-out. Mighty suspicious if you ask me. Plus, they caught a Squad radioing to the outside, probably to that Jack fellow and the Merry Woodsmen. You'll have plenty of time to think about it back at headquarters."

Handcuffed, Gretchen walked outside with her guard. Others gazed and crossed the street to avoid them. A lone motorized chair hummed along.

"But what have I done?" said Gretchen. She gave the Squad a flustered smile.

"Suspicious death, sister, of an Infirm. Was this some kind of revenge?" The Squad's name was Julio. He was part Gypsy, which he was very proud of. His hair was neat, shaved on the sides, and pomaded into something like a scallop shell.

"What? I didn't kill her. She quit breathing. She vomited and then quit breathing."

"Uh huh," said Julio. "Just keep walking."

They passed coffee shops and bars, all empty, and then the Disability Museum. Julio bore right toward Central and the adjoining jail.

"You'll be questioned, so get your story straight," said Julio. Just to check, he said, "Fire and ladder, pronto."

Gretchen looked puzzled.

"Eyes on the prize," said Julio.

Three more blocks and the building had a blinking red J on the front. Julio marched her inside and handed her over to be booked. She was strip-searched, given a red uniform with white stripes on the pants, and led through two locked doors to a hallway of cells with large Chatties on the wall. It was a nature show, a glacier in the process of flipping over. A guard walked toward them, Gomer with his potbelly.

"Well, well, aren't you pretty?" said Gomer. He unpocketed his keys and opened the cell next to

Lura and Mae. "In you go."

"But I haven't done anything. This is unfair," said Gretchen.

"Yeah, well, tell that to your cellmate. Look, she's all ears." Gomer chuckled. "Hey, Bessie Marie! Wakenzie upzie. You got company." He pushed Gretchen inside. "She bites, so be careful."

Bessie Marie lay on her back on the lower bunk, her head and shoulders against the wall, with a blank stare. She was muscled like a man, it seemed to Gretchen.

"Got any drugs?" said Bessie Marie. "Hide 'em in your hidey hole?" Bessie Marie had dark brown hair that looked like a wig, curly and following her ears.

"No. Why would I?" Gretchen couldn't bring herself to move and just stood in one place.

Bessie Marie laughed. "You are wet behind the ears. You like your Champy, right? Well, no Champy in here unless you want to fuck Gomer. Once was enough for me."

"What about food?" said Gretchen.

"Yeah, Scrumptious, but I guess you were expecting something else?" She held out her hand. "Bessie Marie."

Gretchen shook it. "Gretchen."

Mae called from the next cell. "Hey, Bessie Marie. Who we got? Anybody useful?"

"Just an innocent baby girl," said Bessie Marie. "Real pretty, though. So why are you in?"

"My patient died. She quit breathing. I guess they think I killed her, but I didn't. Something about high alert." Gretchen eyed the metal toilet, the little sink cluttered with a toothbrush and cups. The vague sound of air whooshing.

"Huh," said Bessie Marie. "Yeah, Squad's on pins and needles. Something's going down. Killed an Infirm. How about that?"

"No," said Gretchen. "She died on her own. She's missing a leg, and the other one is disabled. Why are you here?"

"Stealing, they say, Champy and other things of necessity. Can't believe they put a murderer in my cell. You don't look the part."

"God," said Gretchen. "Look, is that my bed? Over yours? I need to lie down."

Bessie Marie called out to Mae. "She snuffed one this morning!"

"Hey, good work, baby girl!" said Mae. "We need more of that!"

Gretchen felt dizzy and sat on the toilet rim. She stood and looked for a clean cup. "Mind if I use this cup?"

"Well, sweetie, go ahead. I don't want you killing me in my sleep. Got my eye on you." She laughed.

Gretchen ran a cup of water, drank it, and then another. She watched as Gomer passed, his eyes glued to her. "Going up." She climbed the short ladder to her bunk. There was no pillow or sheet. She lay on her back and stared at the off-white ceiling.

~

The judge, Chet Spurlock, sat in his wheelchair, letting his Upright groom him. She was tweezing hairs from his ears. He snapped his lobster-claw fingers and told her to hurry up. He was getting ready to sentence Lura on live Chatty. The Upright combed his hair with a splash of water, parting it on the side. Early that morning, he'd undergone dialysis and felt puny as a result, but nothing could spoil his day.

Wearing compression hose on his leg stumps and dressed in a white shirt and a black jacket, he motored down the hall, his Upright trailing behind, to meet Cornelius Fava, who would be at his side to give the sentencing more gravity. The door to Conference Room A opened with a hum and swung out. The judge entered. Cornelius Fava was there waiting for him.

"Well, I do declare," said Fava. "The judge is dressed to kill." He laughed and extended his withered hand to shake the judge's lobster-claw.

"Good one, Fava. Let's get this show on the road." He glanced at the clock, eleven on the dot. The Uprights would be cutting toenails.

They positioned themselves in front of a camera in the open room. An Upright was in charge of broadcasting, and he focused the wide-angle lens on the pair. "When you're ready, gentlemen," he said. On the wall, the Chatty played the news, the weather forecast for the next seven days. Lows in the thirties, highs in the forties.

For more impact, the judge had his Upright undo his pants and expose his new flesh-like penis that was fully erect at rest. He asked Fava if he wanted to touch it, but he declined.

"Okay, sixty seconds, and let's get on with it," said the judge.

The cameraman watched the seconds tick by

on the clock and then hit the transmission button. Behind him, the screen changed to the judge with Cornelius to his right. All channels would be interrupted for the sentencing.

The judge smiled. "Well, good morning, citizens of Pan. Today, we are gathered here with the honorable Chief of Central, Cornelius Fava. As you well know, an insufferable crime was committed in which I was the unfortunate recipient. Said crime occurred on November 10, a mere seven days ago, but as you can see, I have been fully restored to my former self with some improvements." At that, he reached for his artificial member and patted it gently. I guess you could say that I've taken lemons and made lemonade. There were two insidious creatures involved in this crime, one who remains at large but not for long. He is the primary criminal, the butcher you might say, but we have in custody his unfortunate accomplice."

The Chatty threw up the faces of Jack and Lura, then resumed with its focus on the judge.

"We all know what the penalty is for harm brought to an Infirm, and that would be a sentence of death." He paused and glanced at Fava, who was nodding his head in agreement. "As such, I hereby sentence Lura to execution by hanging." He paused. "Now, this should come as no surprise. There have been rumors of trouble to follow this expected announcement, but out of the fear of swift and total reprisal, I ask the citizens, the Uprights of Pan, to refrain from acting in any untoward manner. Pan is a peaceful dome, and it shall remain that way. Said execution will take place tomorrow, Tuesday, November eighteen. You shall all have the pleasure of witnessing the timely and deserved punishment at seven a.m. Bath day will go as scheduled, followed by lunch. That is all."

"That is all," said Fava.

The cameraman counted to ten and ceased the live transmission, puddled sweat in his eyebrows. The Chatty reverted to the news, which had already begun analyzing the judge's remarks. An expert panel was waiting in the wings.

"Well, I say that went mighty well," said Fava.

"Yes, indeed. Business as usual," said the judge, zipping his pants. "Juice to celebrate?"

Cornelius licked his lips, and they were off to a juice bar, their respective Uprights in tow.

~

The sun loomed high overhead, tilted toward the south. The helicopter was approaching, beating the air like mashed potatoes. Jack, Bard, and Ismael scurried into the cave. With the two-way, Chad made contact.

"Ground here. Any news? Did you bring supplies? No sign of the fugitives, but we're expecting them to make a move at nightfall. Over."

The helicopter hovered a hundred feet above the pines. "Yep, she received death, today at eleven hundred. Imperative that we catch the bad guys. The judge is impatient. Execution bright and early at 0700 tomorrow. Trouble expected. Dropping supplies, over."

The winch lowered a sack containing Scrumptious and two blankets. Davies retrieved it and loosed the cable.

"Clear," said Chad. "Supplies on the ground. You doing another sweep? Over."

"Yeah, probably do circles in this area, if you think they're nearby, over."

"Sounds good," said Chad. "We'll keep our eyes peeled. If you don't see us, we'll be in the cave, preparing the trap, over."

"Over and out," said the pilot, and off he went.

"Shit, death," said Davies. "What's next?"

"We have to move quick," said Chad. He waited, then trotted to the cave and went to his belly, crawling into the dim chamber. Davies followed.

"Well," said Chad. "The news is in. The judge sentenced her to death. Sentence to be carried out tomorrow at 0700. He mentioned that trouble was expected."

"Hot dog," said Bard. "Plan A. Are we clear?"

"Yeah, plan A. Rescue Lura," said Jack.

"The copter will most likely return sometime this afternoon. Take it then?" said Chad.

"Yeah," said Bard. "But they'll have to land. You inform them that we're caught, ready to be flown back to Pan. Hell, we have to let the insiders know that we're coming. Have to risk using the radio."

"Is this really going to work?" said Davies.

"There he goes," said Ismael. "I say we leave Davies behind."

"No, he's good for it. Right, buddy," said Chad.

"I'm in," said Davies. "Maybe we should leave Ismael behind." He smirked.

Jack stood. "We're in this together. We need all the help we can get." He imagined holding Lura in his arms.

"He's right," said Bard. "Safe to go outside? This cave wears on me."

"Should be," said Chad, and he led the way.

~

In her cell, Lura had watched the whole proceeding on the Chatty in the hallway. Mae tried to comfort her, but Lura crawled onto her bunk in disbelief and curled into a ball.

"Look, babydoll, it's just a ruse. It's some kind of game, I'm sure," said Mae. She reached and rubbed Lura's back. "There hasn't been an execution in ten years. The judge is bluffing. I won't let them take you out of the cell."

Lura bemoaned the day she had laid eyes on Jack. "Fuck. Fuck me," and she wept.

Gomer sidled up to the cell, whistling. "You done it now, young thing." He paused, his hand in his pocket. "Hey, got some Champy here. Take the edge off."

Mae walked to the bars and took the baggie containing four lozenges. "Aw, that's sweet of you, honey."

Gomer puffed up and turned red. He resumed whistling and walking the hall. On the Chatty, a volcano was erupting, hot red lava flowing like burned marshmallows.

"Lura, got you some dope." She dropped a lozenge in a cup of water and watched it fizz. "Lura!"

Lura turned, her eyes red and wet. She swung

her legs over and took the cup, smelling the foamy citrus. "Thanks." She drank, swirled the water in the cup, and drank the rest. Within minutes, the cell began to expand and contract with weird purple colors. Little gnomes passed through the walls, singing a song in a language she didn't recognize. She went to her back and let the visions take over, her face relaxing.

Mae fixed herself a cocktail and drank, taking sips. She could tell that she would be sleeping soon and went to her bed. Her toes tingled, and a warmth enveloped her.

"Hey!" called Bessie Marie from the cell next door. "Mind sharing some of that!" Gretchen was sitting on the lower bunk, not sure what was going on. She figured that if Lura got death, so would she.

There was no response. "Damn," said Bessie Marie. "They're already out, lucky bastards."

"Where will they hang her?" said Gretchen. The words didn't seem to fit in her mouth, as if they were blocks of wood.

"Probably in the damn street. Not sure. Hey Gomer!"

Gomer took his time but walked over. "What?"

"How about some Champy? You got some more? You seem to be in a generous mood today."

"Ha, well, it's not every day that someone gets death. Wait your turn." He touched his stun gun and walked away.

Bessie Marie turned to Gretchen. "If we let him do a three-way, he might hand it over. What do you say?"

"Are you kidding?" said Gretchen.

"Do I look like I'm kidding?" said Bessie Marie. "Come on. It's now or never. It's not so bad. Just pretend like it's sex day. At least it's not with an Infirm."

Gretchen thought. She could use the high. "Maybe we can get him to take some, then take his keys, get out of here."

"Damn, he's not that stupid," said Bessie Marie.

"Maybe he is," said Gretchen.

"We still would have to get past the other guards. It's not like there's a playground on the other side of that door."

"I'll do it," said Gretchen. "I hate to say it, but I've got a great body." She laughed a small laugh. "I think I can turn him."

"What? I'm not a looker?" said Bessie Marie. She was buxom, but her boobs sagged to her waist like two water balloons.

"Just get him back over here," said Gretchen. To add to her sincerity, she pulled off her top, exposing her breasts that turned up, ending in large pink nipples.

"Oh, baby, you got the goods. Hey, Gomer!"

Gomer walked as slowly as he could, standing in front of their cell without looking in. "What? You got an offer on the table?" He glanced and then saw Gretchen topless. "Shit."

"Let's do a quick three-way. She's in. For the Champy. How about it?"

Gomer swallowed, glancing at the Chatty. His antics were tolerated to some extent, but he could still get in hot water messing with the inmates.

"Well, okay." He was as hard as a rock. "Get naked, both of you, and hurry."

Gretchen was already sliding off her pants and panties. Bessie Marie followed suit until they were both standing there buck naked.

"What you waiting on?" said Bessie Marie.

Gomer looked as if he was floating. He took the key and opened the cell door, unzipping his pants. He stepped in, enthralled by Gretchen's V of pubic hair. He'd had Bessie Marie, and that was old news.

"One thing," said Gretchen. "You take some Champy with us." She spread her legs a bit.

"You're joking," said Gomer. He pulled his throbbing member through his zipper.

"Yeah, look at that, baby boy," said Bessie Marie. "Come on, just a few sips. It'll be fun."

"But we fuck first," said Gomer. He watched Bessie Marie draw up three cups of water. He reached into his pocket for a baggie, pulled it out, and handed it to her. She dropped a lozenge into each one.

"Come on, sailor," said Gretchen. She bent over, showing him her smooth backside.

Gomer swallowed and grabbed her hips. She had to help him enter, and he gasped, soon thrusting and coming within thirty seconds. Without hesitating, he took one of the cups and drank half, his hands groping Gretchen's breasts. She let him have his fun while Bessie Marie rubbed against him.

"Now, drink the rest," said Gretchen.

Gomer did as he was told, in a trance. Already, the room was beginning to squirm. He caught himself from falling and muttered, "Shit." With his dick still protruding from his pants, he staggered to the cell door and let himself out. He slammed the door shut, wobbled to his chair in the middle of the hallway, and sat down hard, staring into a void filled with unguent colors.

"Ha, what a dope," said Bessie Marie. "You did great, baby girl." She reached for a cup of Champy and downed it. Her eyes grew heavy, and she drifted to her bunk still naked.

Gomer's keys in hand, Gretchen could feel the weight of the world on her shoulders and dressed. She took the cup of Champy, eager to be more stoned than free, and drank. A rush of heat enveloped her body, and she barely made it to her bunk.

~

The news of the impending execution of Lura spread like herpes throughout the dome. Two Squad, Remy and Kate, had been arrested for illicit radio contact with the outside. Whispers and nods and sign language. Instead of reporting to shower time, the Uprights would gather en masse in front of Central, demanding that the execution be called off, that Lura be set free. They would stand as one and not disperse, taking their grievance throughout the night and into bath and lunch day. The bistros would be empty, the Infirm unwashed. Fifty-two was ecstatic. He was meeting Mariah at the Disability Museum before the big showdown. The Infirm were going down.

~

With the helicopter droning in and out, the guys sat and talked, fine-tuning their plans. What if the helicopter crashed? What then? Then we go in through the sewer. But what if it was guarded? We shoot our way through. Stun grenades, a sack full. The conversation circled and circled, but no one had a clear idea of exactly how they would free Lura. That would just have to come of its own accord.

Jack cleaned his teeth with a twig. His stomach was in knots. The scheduled radio contact at 1700 had come and gone. Nothing. And now the helicopter seemed to have disappeared. He listened so hard that his head hurt, willing it to come to them. Lura would be dead within fifteen hours.

"So, what the hell could be going on in there?" said Davies. "Do you really think there'll be riots? I mean, great if they do."

"This has been a long time coming, partner," said Bard. "Since we left the dome six months ago, this is just what we've been agitating for, like a prophecy in the making. If the Uprights don't create a diversion, then I should just shoot myself, call it a day, a life."

Ismael nodded. "Nothing like being on the run and hunted. Whatever happens happens. The Infirm, goddamn them."

"Yeah," said Jack. "I followed you guys on the Chatty. God, you had the expert panels in an uproar. They always ended by saying you would be caught the next day, and then the next. Had conversations at the Disability Museum. Whispers in the street. Now that I look back on it, the little threads are coming together. I never thought I'd be the trigger, or rather, Lura. I just wish I were in her spot." He paced to and fro, scanning the ground, stepping around ants, listening for the helicopter.

"God," said Chad. "I feel like my whole body's a boner." He laughed and coughed. "I say we have a bite to eat. The copter should be coming any minute. They don't fly after dark."

And there it was, a faint chopping of the air, like a staple gun gone crazy.

They fell into line, Bard, Jack, and Ismael sitting on the ground. Chad and Davies with guns drawn. Chad waited until the noise was within half a mile. He spotted the red craft through the tops of the pines. He had to convince them to land.

"Ground to air! Ground to air! Mission accomplished. We got the scoundrels. Need assistance with evacuation. Over!" Chad waited, but there was only static for five seconds."

"You're fucking kidding," said the pilot. He zoned in on the ridgeline and spotted the group on the ground. He would have to land on one of the enormous boulders, tricky. He turned and gave a thumbs up to the two Squad in back. "Air to ground. Going to land this beast just uphill from your location. Over."

"Copy," said Chad. "We'll head that way with our catch. You'll need to drop your Squad, though, and come back for them. Over."

"They're armed," said the pilot. He licked his buck teeth. "Just hand 'em over. I'll come back if there's daylight, but otherwise, you have to spend the night. Congrats. Over."

"Damn," said Chad. "Davies, we'll have to take

Squad. Force them out." He spoke to the pilot. "Copy, will do. Over. But they're slippery creatures. Over."

"Copy," said the pilot. He paused above the trees and eased the machine down with a clearance of some fifty feet in a rough circle. He tapped the rock and rose and then tapped again, bringing down the rpms. "Okay, come on. Don't get your heads cut off. Over."

With pistols drawn, Chad and Davies ordered Jack, Bard, and Ismael to put their hands behind their heads. They left the cuffs off. Single file, they walked uphill through small boulders, soon entering the downwash of the copter. The two Squad had exited and were high-fiving one another with big grins and pistols out. Chad gave them a wave and a big smile. He glanced over at Davies and winked. "Hold it steady."

They had to ascend a natural rock staircase, using their hands and feet. Jack was first up and, bent over, made his way to the open cargo door. The Squad yelled at him to get in, and he did, followed by Bard, and then Ismael. They sat in the vibrating craft with their heads down as if ashamed of all the trouble they had created. The other Squad was on the far side and had entered and closed that door. It was now or never, and Chad jumped in.

It was crowded inside. The pilot sat at his controls, glancing back but holding the machine in place.

"Help me cuff them," said Chad over the roar. He maneuvered behind the Squad, who was pulling cuffs from his belt. At the right moment, he shoved the Squad, sending him headfirst through the door and off the giant boulder. The Squad outside looked dumbfounded as Davies held his pistol five feet from his head, motioning for him to get down, and then leaped into the copter.

Chad grabbed the sliding door and yanked it shut. Bard was up, leaning into the cockpit, ripping the headset from the pilot's head.

"The fuck!" said the pilot. The copter wobbled, lifted, and hit with a thud, the skid coming down on the Squad's foot, breaking it. The pilot's eyes seemed like lost marbles as he watched Chad scramble over and into the seat beside him, pistol drawn and beaded on his head. "What the hell are you doing!"

"Just shut up and get in the air, head to the dome!" For effect, he fired a round past the pilot's head into the Plexiglas window, making a hole as big as two fingers.

"Are you crazy!"

"Yes! And you're an Upright, just like me. We're in this together, good buddy. Play your cards right, and you can be a hero. You know you hate the Infirm. Now fly!"

The pilot hesitated, drinking it in. He throttled up, and the copter lifted, doing a slow spin until clear of the trees. He muttered and flew, headed in the wrong direction.

"To the dome, asshole!" said Chad. He checked behind him, and the guys were all grins.

The pilot did as he was told and took a long, slow arc, headed to Pan.

~

In Pan, Squad was hopping. Fresh reports of shower no-shows were pouring in, fifty-three in all, and all reserves were being summoned. The priority was to secure and protect members of Central. A dozen Squad members were already there, dressed in riot gear with shields and stun grenades. Cornelius Fava was preparing to go live and issue a call for calm. He'd spoken with the judge about the new plan for Lura, and at least that seemed to be on track. With his head drawn to his shoulder, he practiced what he would say.

At the dome's jail, another dozen Squad had gathered, a few with pistols. Inside her cell, Lura sat, leaning against the wall. The gnomes were still there, building little horses from wires and sand. Below her, Mae snored the sleep of the dead. In the next cell, Bessie Marie slept as well, and Gretchen watched as the oozing colors became snakes, which became butterflies, which became snakes. In his chair in the hallway, Gomer had descended into a deep river gorge, the deepest in South America, in Peru. He reached out and touched the rock walls, which bled and fed the river.

Below the roads, in a tunnel connecting his building with the jail and Central, the judge was being whisked away by his faithful Upright. The judge wanted to be there, despite the danger. He imagined himself as all-powerful and capable of turning back a tide of Uprights with his lobster-claw hands. "Hurry," he said.

~

The flight back to Pan only took thirty-five minutes. The pilot had no way to communicate with ground and wondered if the entrance panels were withdrawn or closed. Thoughts of crashing the machine crossed his mind, but he wanted to live. "I need the headset!"

Chad pondered his options. He had no idea what the protocol for landing was, whether they could get in without permission from the dome. He handed the headset to the pilot. "Keep it real! You're doing this for your own kind. Got it! I'd just as soon shoot you as a traitor otherwise! Got it!"

"Got it," mouthed the pilot. The dome was in sight, rising like a cloudy blister. The helicopter portal was on the west side, and he could see that it was open. A windsock showed a slight breeze. "Permission to land. Over. Prisoners on board. I repeat, prisoners on board. Over."

The pilot circled once and maneuvered to hover. The panels were partially open and began retracting as he lowered slowly. A bright orange helipad was just there with a big black X.

The guys in back waited, strung like piano wire. They had a plan, but it seemed foggy now that it was actually happening. They had to make it to the jail, spring Lura, and somehow get her out without getting caught. They gave each other grim but encouraging looks.

The copter spun from left to right and lowered inside the dome, still a hundred feet from the ground. The pilot took it down, and soon they were on the helipad.

The pilot glanced at Chad.

"Keep it running, doughboy," said Chad. "And tell them to keep the panels open, that you have to go back and fetch equipment." He listened as the pilot did as he was told.

Chad leaned into the back. "Change of plans. Davies, you stay here with the pilot, keep him covered. Us three will go in. With any luck, we'll be back with Lura and fly back out. Got it?"

"Got it!"

They changed places, Chad keeping his pistol aimed at the pilot. Davies took the seat, a look of consternation on his face.

"Okay, fellas, it's now or never." Chad slid the door open and jumped down. Jack, Bard, and Ismael followed, each carrying a stun grenade. There was a gate out, guarded by two Squad who were looking on with interest. As planned, Chad walked behind the trio, their hands held behind their heads.

"Open the gate!" Chad spoke with authority, a look of annoyance on his face. "Gotta get these guys booked."

"Not gonna take a cart? It's a good ten blocks to the jail, said one of the guards.

"Nope, gonna make 'em walk. Now open the gate."

The two guards looked at one another and shrugged. The gate rolled open.

Once in the street, they walked for a block down the empty street. The final rays of sunshine washed the bland buildings, and then they broke into a trot and then into a run, passing scanners along the way. A hover-head zoomed around a corner and followed them, sending a live feed into Squad.

~

The judge and his Upright rode the elevator to the first floor of the jail, meeting there with the warden. He was against their plan, but could do nothing to stop them. He paired them with a guard who carried a sheet and watched as they re-entered the elevator and rode to the second floor. There the three exited, the Upright trembling at what was about to take place. The first station guard opened the heavy steel door and let them through into the first hallway of cells. A few inmates, glimpsing the entourage, called down curses on the judge, who visibly winced, wanting to put them out of their sweet misery. "Quick now," said the judge. He was feeling woozy, in need of another round of dialysis, but that would come soon enough in the morning.

At the second metal door, they waited for Gomer to let them in. No one came, and the guard peered through the small glass window and saw Gomer half sitting in his chair in the hall. "That's weird," he said.

~

The four covered ten blocks in less than ten minutes, with half a dozen hover-heads in pursuit. Chad motioned for them to stop and peered around the corner of an Upright section of flats. The jail was a block away, and he could see gathered there about twenty Squad in their riot gear.

"Okay, now we switch." Chad handed his pistol

to Bard and put his hands behind his head.

The three marched behind Chad, soon drawing the attention of the group of Squad. One broke away to investigate. "What's this? That you, Chad?"

"You've got to let us through. They shot Davies, and they'll shoot me. They just want to talk with Lura, say goodbye, and then they'll give themselves up."

Two more Squad had approached. One said, "Holy cow, Bard and Ismael? Chad?"

"Well, hey there, fellas," said Bard. "Jerry." He tipped an imaginary hat.

"Gentlemen," said Ismael.

"The Merry Woodsmen," said Jerry, as if addressing Jerry Lewis himself.

"Let us through," said Chad. "They'll shoot otherwise. I want to live." He walked forward, the gun in Bard's hand to the back of his head, and the Squad parted, whispers passing among them.

Jerry held the door open for them, entranced, and yelled for the tubby man behind the desk to release the door into the jail proper.

The guard fumbled for his key and let the judge, his Upright, and the other guard pass through into the cell block. He made a beeline for Gomer and slapped him around, trying to make sense of the scene.

"Which cell, Lura?" said the judge, his eyes greedy with large, dilated pupils. He'd braced himself with a nip of alcohol and needed another drink.

The guard pointed. "Here. Hey, Lura! You have

a visitor." He had no idea what was happening and turned back to Gomer.

"No, fool, forget about him. Open her cell. We have a little surprise for the missus."

The guard found the key and opened the cell. Lura was on the top bunk, lost in the velvet of her Champy trance. He pushed the sheet over a top bar of the cell door and then tried to rouse Lura.

"Get her down, now," said the judge.

The guard dragged Lura from the top bunk, nearly dropping her. He managed to make her stand, but had to pull her over to the bars.

Still at gunpoint, Chad led the way, talking his way past the guard at the elevator. "It's okay, buddy. Once they see Lura, they're all mine. The tables turn. I promise. So, what floor for Lura?"

The guard there, a rakish man with a three-day beard and sunken eyes, said "Two," and then he was on the phone.

On two, they exited.

"Jesus, what next?" said the guard who had let the judge pass not five minutes earlier.

"Lura. Making a visit. They'll shoot me. They shot Davies. Once they see her, they'll give the gun to me." Chad tried to make his voice tremble. "Follow if you want, but open the next door."

The guard hit the door release and then walked that way to unlock the lock, and in they walked to the first hall of cells. One more door to go.

With the sheet tied around Lura's neck, the guard

closed the cell door, holding onto the other end through the bars.

"Raise her up on her tippy toes," said the judge. He smiled.

The guard pulled on the sheet, and Lura straightened. The guard pulled harder, and Lura rose a few inches, her breath catching, and she began to gasp. The guard put his body into it, and Lura's toes barely touched the hard floor. He struggled to wind the sheet around the bar and managed a rough knot as Lura choked. Her death would be ruled a suicide. Sweating, he stood back, and the door burst open.

Jack was first in. He ran to the cell, ramming the judge's wheelchair, sending him sprawling to the floor. Bard moved his pistol back and forth, covering the two guards. One reached for his stun gun, and Bard shot him in the foot, a cry of agony.

"Need help!" said Jack. "Open the goddamned cell!" He struggled with the sheet to no avail. Lura was turning purple.

"You, open the cell!" said Bard.

The guard lurched forward, his keys clattering to the floor.

Jack reached through the bars and grabbed Lura beneath her armpits and lifted with all his might. The guard finally got the key and opened the cell. Chad rushed in and lifted Lura as Jack got busy unfastening the knot. Lura collapsed, her breathing jagged and loud. The gnomes had attacked her, dragging her behind a magical bus by her neck. She moaned and coughed.

A group of Squad entered. Ismael unleashed a stun grenade. The device exploded, scattering them. All hell broke loose, and Bard hefted Lura onto his broad shoulders and plowed forward, handing the pistol to Chad.

At the next door, they paused, and it magically opened. On their way to the elevator, Chad said, "Thanks, mate!" and soon they reached the first floor. One more door to go, and it too opened, and they were outside amid a hubbub of Squad who were beginning to deal with a crowd of Uprights that had gathered in silence. They didn't quite know what to do and watched as Chad held the pistol on Bard, who was carrying Lura, and on Ismael and Jack, who had their hands raised in the air. The crowd of Uprights and Squad parted, but soon half a dozen Squad followed as Bard led the way, wheezing under the weight of Lura. Jack glanced back, pulled the pin on a stun grenade, and tossed it over his shoulder. The grenade exploded, slowing the progress of their pursuers, and on they ran, then trotted, Bard slowing with his burden. Halfway there, Bard had to rest.

"Need help, Jack."

Jack took Lura from Bard, and off they went again, another stun grenade thrown by Bard. A shot rang out and then another. Chad turned and fired over their heads. They were within three blocks of the helipad, and coming toward them was Davies, his gun drawn. There was no helicopter sound.

"Halt!" said Davies. He trained his pistol on Bard.

"You fucking idiot!" said Chad, pistol raised. They both fired simultaneously, hitting Chad in the arm. He stopped, knelt, and fired, hitting Davies in the leg. He spun and dropped his pistol.

"The sewer! To the park!" said Jack, and Bard was in the lead, turning right. For five minutes, they ran, but Jack slowed, and Ismael took Lura. She was moaning and beginning to struggle.

Past rows of Upright buildings, a mini theater, and within five minutes, they were at the vast park with its scattering of gingko trees. Light was fading into twilight, and they plunged forward. Shots fired. Chad glanced at his bleeding arm, turned, and fired into the small crowd pursuing them.

They crossed a road and then a shallow culvert, passed a pond, and then Ismael went flying over a bench, dropping Lura. They regrouped, Jack taking the lead and Lura, feeling superhuman strength with his precious cargo. They were on a road covered with leaves. Jack knew the manhole was near and recognized the place. "Here!"

Bard lifted the cover and tossed it aside. Down he went, followed by Chad. Jack unloaded Lura and placed her legs in the gaping black hole. Ismael stood ready with a grenade. "Hurry! Get down!" he said.

Jack, determined not to leave Lura behind a second time, lowered her into the hole and let her go into the waiting arms of Chad. Shots fired, and Ismael fell, blood spurting from his head. Jack paused, remembered Lura, cursed, then disappeared down the hole.

~

Screeching on the floor, the judge soon became the focus at the jail, heads hung in shame for show, all hands attentive to his needs. Back in his wheelchair, he nursed a sore shoulder and a broken thumb on his lobster-claw hand. He realized what had happened, that he'd been had, yelling this order and that, and he was returned to his flat where he spent the sleepless night plotting his next move with the members of Central.

Outside in the streets, the Uprights were on the move, chanting the name: "Lura! Lura!" and there would be no bath day, no sex day, just a day of reckoning, the Infirm be damned.

9 781943 661244